RAINBOW OF LOVE

When Paul Melandes sailed his yacht into St Peter Port harbour, Guernsey, he sailed into Sorelle Dalby's heart. His yacht was called the *Privateer*. Was its owner a seeker of romantic treasure, a collector of hearts? Would he slip away one dawn on a new quest, or would he hand her the key to her own new-found treasure trove — himself? Disappointment, anger, depression, near tragedy and an island lie on Sorelle's horizon. Can she steer a course to that happiness beyond?

LLOYD PETERS

RAINBOW OF LOVE

Complete and Unabridged

LINFORD
Leicester

First published in Great Britain in 1989

First Linford Edition
published 2004

British Library CIP Data

Peters, Lloyd
    Rainbow of love.—Large print ed.—
Linford romance library
    1. Love stories
    2. Large type books
    I. Title
    823.9'14 [F]

ISBN 1–84395–327–7

Published by
F. A. Thorpe (Publishing)
Anstey, Leicestershire

Set by Words & Graphics Ltd.
Anstey, Leicestershire
Printed and bound in Great Britain by
T. J. International Ltd., Padstow, Cornwall

This book is printed on acid-free paper

1

Sorelle's gaze wandered idly over the harbour. At the castle, the boats, the distant islands. The jetties with their rows of parked cars. Behind her the noise of traffic, the press and bustle of people along the esplanade walk.

She became aware of a yacht passing between the walls of the outer harbour. Watched its approach to the inner one, a diminishing bow-wave telling of its slowing progress through the water. Sorelle screwed up her eyes against the sun. The boat was white and large with a vivid blue waterline — a beautiful, graceful thing. She could just make out the name in blue letters — *Privateer*. Didn't recognise the name nor the boat. It had a buccaneering sound to it. Another visitor, she guessed.

The yacht was being berthed expertly against the jetty wall to Sorelle's left.

She could see two men and a dark-haired woman on the deck. A third man was at the wheel, bronzed-face showing vividly against his white cap and shirt as he directed the operation commandingly but quietly.

Glancing at her watch she saw that it was time to return to the hotel where she worked as a receptionist — the Longchamps being acknowledged as the best on the island. She started to make her way to the crossing further on, a slender yet curvaceous figure in a black-pleated skirt and a white half-sleeved blouse, her fair loosely curled hair burnished brighter by the sun.

Suddenly a man appeared over the topmost rung of the iron steps used by boat people to reach the esplanade. He collided with her, sending her staggering. But almost at once she felt herself grasped then pulled upright again, warm hands pressing into the middle of her back.

She looked up. He was tall into the blue sky like the masts of the

2

yachts behind him. White-capped, white-shirted, his shoulders blotting out the harbour. Bronze flesh through the open cloth, the smell of masculinity and the sea. His eyes held hers. Disbelief, the shadow of a wince in them. Fleeting seconds, then an apologetic smile affording a glimpse of white teeth changed the look.

He let her go. 'Sorry, young lady — clumsy of me. It's what comes of stepping straight from deck to shore. Not hurt?' The voice was American, low, resonant, sending delicious feelings through her.

'No,' she shook her head smiling up at him. 'I'm all right, thank you.' The two of them an island with the rest of the world going around them.

'Sure?' His eyes enveloped her.

Unwillingly she tore her own away, nodded her thanks again and turned to join the group of people waiting at the traffic lights. When their eyes had met a lightning strike hit her somewhere between the pit of her stomach and the top of her thighs. No man had ever given a shock like that to her senses before.

She tried to steady her thoughts as she walked up the old steps between the buildings into High Street. He had mistaken her for someone else at first — of that she was sure. His sudden strange expression. A jingle came into her mind. All the threes — thirty-three. He would be about that. By the time she reached the hotel she had formed a mental picture of him. Dark hair, hazel eyes, about six-four, white shirt, sand coloured slacks. Their encounter had occurred so swiftly that she had no time to notice any further details about him but those she had made a lasting impression upon her.

In the hotel foyer, John the commissionaire, portly and in grey uniform, gave her a small salute in greeting, a genial Father Christmas in a different coloured suit, she thought.

'Anything exciting happened? No royalty, heads of state arrived?'

'No, plenty of arrivals but no celebrities.'

'Oh well, can't have them every week,' she smiled back over her shoulder.

By three o'clock precisely she was behind reception. Three till midnight then the next day off. She scanned the list of guests yet to come that day. Several off the four o'clock plane from the mainland. Three from Jersey at four-thirty. A couple from Paris at three-thirty, and two from the boat at six o'clock.

It was cooler in the foyer, noise and light subdued with the occasional sounds of laughter and splashes from the pool, voices and the tinkle of crockery from the lounge. Must be nice, she thought, to be rich enough to do what you wanted — when you wanted. She envied the holiday guests sometimes, but then would tell herself that she was lucky — living on the island of Guernsey. Had been born there but had left when very young with her parents, her father having found work elsewhere. He had died suddenly some years ago leaving her mother to bring up *she* and her brother Tony.

Over the years the urge to return to her birth-place again had grown stronger and three years ago she had come, found her present job and had stayed. Tony had remained at home unmarried.

For the first hour she was busy with no time for her thoughts to stray, but then after seeing the latest arrivals disappear into the lift with one of the porters, her mind drifted back to the stranger who had collided with her on the harbour walk. She had a feeling that he was off the large yacht — the *Privateer* she had seen berthing. He was probably the same man she had seen at its helm. Remembered him saying that he had just stepped ashore.

The telephone rang, jerking her back into the present again. 'The Longchamps Hotel.'

'I want a table for five for dinner tonight, please.' An American male voice. Firm, polite, yet bearing the tone of a man used to having his requests carried out. The same man — the object of her thoughts moments before. She was sure. Her pulse raced. The same sensations in her body.

'Hello.'

Sorelle pulled herself together. 'Y-yes, sir. One moment please. Oh, what time, sir?' She knew she did not sound efficient.

'Nine o'clock.' She guessed that he too did not think so.

She rang through to the restaurant. Hoped Marcel the head waiter could manage. He could.

'Yes, sir. Nine o'clock for five.' She forced herself to be extra businesslike. 'What name, sir?'

'Melandes. Paul Melandes.'

'Thank you, Mr Melandes.' She put the phone down slowly. Melandes. She'd heard the name before. Fashion? Oil? Films? Something to do with clothes, nearly certain. She shrugged. It was not forced to be the same man. Yet the feeling persisted that it was. The voice . . . Despite the effect he'd had on her, she wasn't sure that she wanted him to see her behind the reception desk. She had after all sounded like a bumbling juvenile on the telephone with him. Anyway, she told herself, why was she thinking about him? An attractive man like that would have been snapped up long ago. Probably married with children. And no doubt his life-style would be rather different to hers.

Nevertheless as nine o'clock approached Sorelle found herself glancing in the direction of the main doors. Earlier she had found out from Patti le Bourg, manageress of the hotel's boutique, that Paul Melandes was the name in shoes, leather goods and clothing accessories. His products world-wide with factories in the U.S.A. and Europe, and, she had informed Sorelle, they had some of his evening footwear in stock. Intrigued, Sorelle had left her desk for a hurried look. Fabulous creations and expensive they were — almost a week's salary, with nearby the *haute couture* of Paris and London to go with them.

In the event she was almost caught unawares, looking up from the register just in time to see a party of two women and three men coming through the foyer. It was the man in the white dinner jacket that held her attention, she trying hard not to stare. She recognised him as the same man who had bumped into her. Now he was immaculately groomed, dark-haired, bronzed, body narrowing from wide shoulders to narrow hips under the superb cut of his jacket, the cast of his face serious and proud. Walking with an easy ranging gait. By his side was a self-assured looking red-haired woman in her late twenties, wearing a long green evening dress. With them were a dark-haired woman of about thirty-five, an older greying man, and a slim younger man.

Sorelle saw him glance about him casually. His eyes met hers again, the same shadow of some past hurt flickered over his features. A slight frown, then his recognition of her. His lips lengthened. 'Hello again.'

'Good evening, Mr Melandes.' Then he was past. It was him she realised and this was confirmed when she heard Marcel, the head waiter, greet him at the entrance to the restaurant. Sorelle had noticed the girl in green's backward dismissive look at her, no doubt wondering how she came to know Mr Paul Melandes. She sighed deeply after them. Would have given anything to have been in that person's place. To spend the evening looking into those deep disturbing eyes.

By eleven o'clock she was beginning to feel tired and just a little miserable. Music was coming from the piano in the restaurant — soft romantic melodies. A couple drifted by her desk hand in hand, intent upon each other, the girl leaning close against her escort. In another hour she would be going home alone to her flat. She'd had boy-friends, but no man had touched her heart and held it, though some had mistaken her straight bluebell blue gaze as an invitation to her bed.

She glanced in the direction of the restaurant, had seen nothing more of Paul Melandes and his party. With a wry smile to herself Sorelle guessed that he would be far too occupied looking into the face of the girl in green to bother about the one behind the reception desk.

The taxi arrived and took her home. It wasn't far to the top of the Grange. She had a small car of her own but the hotel provided the transport for her on the late shift. In the darkness of her bed the face of Paul Melandes with its enfolding, compelling eyes floated above her. She fell asleep looking into them.

Next morning she awoke to the subdued sound of traffic. Summer traffic had a different sound. Perhaps it was the presence of the holiday-makers — a vitality, a bustling which wasn't so evident in the winter. She looked out of her window. Bright sunlight already dappled the tarmac through the trees. Her day off just to do whatever she wanted. She decided to go to her favourite bay situated on the south coast. It was Sunday, a day when the boat-minded fraternity of the island took to their craft. From St. Peter Port an exodus to the neighbouring islands or a shorter sail to the bays nearer at hand.

After breakfast Sorelle put on her bikini. On top of that a short squash-type white skirt with two bands of light and dark blue round the hem, and a matching short-sleeve top. A blue bandanna round her hair and sandals completed her ensemble. In a small holdall she threw a white cardigan, a towel, sun cream and, just in case she stayed out later, a pair of lightweight dark blue slacks.

Driving her red mini she reached the lane leading to Moulin Huet Bay. Passed the Belle Ami Hotel at the top

— an old building set in its own beautiful grounds — a place of elegance and tranquillity. It was cool and shaded under the arch of trees as she went down the winding lane. Close-packed hedges with honeysuckle, a small stream down one side and the occasional well-screened house. Leaving her car in the small car park near the bottom, Sorelle continued on foot down the narrow path towards the bay. Just above the steps leading to the beach was a small tea-garden, a quiet serene place surrounded by rhododendron bushes.

She bought a coffee and sat looking out over the hedge top to the sea beyond. It was going to be a hot day, the mist beginning to clear the Pea Stacks. From her position she could see two yachts riding at anchor and appearing quite small, also the line of the cliff path to Fermain Bay and the distant movement of people upon it.

Afterwards she left the tea-garden and gazed down at the beach. Rocks — some of them huge and of assorted shapes — broke up the sandy part, and people out of sight behind them made it appear less busy than it really was. Bulging cliffs overhung the pebbly rear and the shore shelved gradually, making the beach a safe one to bathe from. A few heads bobbed in the water, some people stood at its edge.

Glancing seawards she noticed another yacht, a large white one swinging gently to anchor some two hundred yards out. It was almost stern on to her, and had not been in view from the tea-garden. The sight of it brought Paul Melandes into her mind. What would he be doing that day? Perhaps having lunch at some sophisticated place with the red-haired girl, or pre-lunch drinks on his yacht in the harbour. Sorelle tried to stop further thoughts of him entering her mind. She had come to that beach to enjoy herself on her day off and she must make the most of it.

On the beach she found a sheltered quiet place, and decided to sunbathe before going for a swim. For the next hour she lay there, the sun growing hotter, hearing the crunch of feet on pebbles, disembodied voices, the sighing of the surf and the occasional drone of a motor boat.

Later she gathered her things and threaded her way between the rocks towards the water. It looked calm and inviting and the tide appeared to be going out. Privacy was afforded by a large rock behind her, one jutting into the sea on her left, and an empty crescent of sand to her right. She stood enjoying the play of the breeze on her body — tanned golden by regular exposure during the summer months. Her bikini was new — blue, purple and yellow diagonal stripes, the bottom half held by two yellow bows at the hips.

Slipping the top off she breathed deeply, enjoying the freedom, then stepped towards the water. A sudden glint of brightness out in the bay caught her attention. From the white yacht anchored there but now more side on to her. Metal flashing perhaps in the sun's glare? Sorelle stood at the water's edge, bare-breasted, one hand shading her eyes.

A dark-haired man on the after deck of the yacht was looking in her direction through binoculars. She half turned thinking he was looking at someone else but there was no-one nearby. Turning seawards again, she saw him lower his glasses and wave at her. Her face flushed under the tan. He must have had a very close view of her half-naked body.

Sorelle waded into the water avoiding looking in his direction. Paused when it was up to her thighs, then quickly immersed the rest of herself. She glanced in the direction of the yacht. The man had gone. She began to swim on her back easily, languidly, looking up into the blue sky. Then she stopped, her body just drifting and relaxed. Something touched her face. Seaweed. Pulling herself upright she saw she was quite close to the yacht which appeared larger than ever from the water, being only about fifty yards away.

It was beginning to swing at its anchorage, the after end moving away from her, but not before she had seen the name on its stern — *Privateer*. Paul Melandes' boat! Was he the man who had been watching her from the deck? At that moment she heard the sound of a motor starting up and from the other side of the yacht a small-cabined boat came into view heading for the beach. Several people were in it but she was unable to recognise anyone from her position in the water. How surprising that his yacht should be anchored in Moulin Huet Bay when she had decided to visit that particular one herself.

She trod water for a few moments watching its progress towards the beach. Tiring somewhat, she tried to touch bottom but found she could not — she was out of her depth. Sorelle did not worry — she was quite a strong swimmer, but told herself that she had been foolish, had forgotten about the ebbing tide. Turning on her back she struck out strongly for the shore. After a few minutes she glanced round. The beach did not seem any nearer and the yacht had not become smaller.

Sorelle was somewhat alarmed. Might it be easier for her to swim back in the yacht's direction and cling to the anchor cable jutting from the water? And yet even though she knew she was in some danger she was reluctant to do that. Because, it being Paul Melandes' boat, she did not want him to think that she was doing it to attract his attention. Instead she tried front crawl towards the shore. She could see the beach and the boat being pulled out of the water. Wished she was with that party — no matter what he or they thought.

Sorelle now realised that she was in real danger, feeling the cold and tiring fast. What an idiot she'd been. Decided to try and reach the anchor cable. Pride must go. She floundered, her arms heavy, the smooth polished strokes gone. Swallowed water, came upright, gasping. She shouted, one arm raised, at the group newly on the beach. Her face went under. She came up, her vision blurred with the salt, and screamed. She glimpsed a dark head moving through the water towards her, powerful strokes cleaving and pulling the swimmer swiftly towards her.

She was conscious of shouted encouragement, masterful arms about her, strong expert placing of her body alongside his. Borne along, mouth clear of the water, then lifted effortlessly, her face against a wet, hairy, hard plateau of male chest. Moments later felt the ground against her back. A mouth pressed to hers. Opened her eyes to stare up into those of Paul Melandes — the latter's holding a terrible anxiety to be replaced instantly by enormous relief.

'All right now?' he asked, water dripping from his body on to hers.

She nodded, made an attempt at an apologetic smile. 'Sorry — stupid of me.' Became aware that she was half naked. Someone passed a towel. The man above her draped it tenderly over her shoulders, covering her breasts. Helped her to sit up.

'Scott,' she heard him order, 'fetch some brandy from the saloon.'

A woman's voice — American. 'There, honey. That'll warm you till the brandy arrives.' A dark-haired woman looked into her face. Sorelle murmured her thanks, but the fingers which guided the cup to her lips were those of a man — Paul Melandes.

Then came the sound of the boat returning again. A bottle replaced the cup.

'Take a good long drink,' Paul Melandes' voice came at her ear supporting her in the crook of his arm. She spluttered as the fiery liquid burned its way down her throat. 'Again,' he insisted.

She complied, but shook her head against more. 'Thank you, I'm better now, I'll be all right.'

The dark-haired woman produced a short beach jacket, helped her into it.

Sorelle knew she must look awful. Undignified, half dressed, and now probably fast becoming drunk on the brandy. She hastened to thank the man who had rescued her, now squatting easily at her side.

'I'm sure I owe my life to you. Thank you very much, Mr . . . ' She paused, knowing who he was, but still frightened that he may think she'd done it on purpose. His eyes were a compelling mixture of grey, green and brown.

'Melandes — Paul.'

She extended her hand. 'Sorelle Dalby.'

'Sorelle.' He sighed her name like a caress causing a tremor of delight to course through her body. He must know that she was the person he had been studying through his binoculars earlier. Still holding her hand he introduced her to the others in his party.

She recognised them as being those who had dined in the hotel the night before. Scott, a lanky fair-haired man of about thirty. An older red-faced grey-ing, stiffish man, Maurice, his wife, Ann, the dark-haired woman, and the red-haired girl in a striking black and red one-piece swim suit, called Margot.

Three pairs of kindly, sympathetic eyes and a fourth unfriendly, regarded her, the latter those of the girl Margot who Sorelle sensed thought her an interloper.

'Miss Dalby and I keep bumping into each other — literally,' Paul Melandes said in amused tones. He stood up, looked down from his great height on her then added banteringly, 'If you had really wanted to see the *Privateer* at close quarters there was an easier way to do it. I should have been delighted to show you over it.'

Sorelle felt herself colouring. He thought she had been hanging around, perhaps hoping for an invitation aboard. She got to her feet unsteadily with an inner indignation. 'I'm sorry for causing you such trouble, I just drifted. I didn't mean to interrupt anything.' She glanced at the woman Anne. 'I'll go and get my clothes then I'll return this,' indicating the beach jacket that the other had given her.

Paul Melandes' warm hand round her upper arm stopped her. 'Please, now you've arrived I insist that you join our beach picnic. It's the least you can do for me seeing that I've saved you. Celebrate your return from a near watery end.' His powerful, enveloping gaze held hers.

She knew she ought to go. Common sense told her so. Leave them to themselves. But she was weak when it came to this man. He caused such sensations that she had never felt before to run through her being. Perhaps this time the brandy was helping also. 'Well, just a while then Mr Melandes,' she agreed.

'Paul.'

'Er, Paul. I've upset your day enough already. I don't want to intrude any more.'

'You won't, one more won't make any difference.'

Sorelle encountered a virulent look from the girl Margot.

Paul picked up a towel, blotted the remaining droplets of water from his body. 'Now, let's eat. That exercise has given me one hell of an appetite.'

Scott and Maurice had already set up a folding table, and the two women busied themselves filling its top with food from a large basket which also held an ice box.

Sorelle dined well but uncomfortably, feeling that she should not have been there. On caviare which she did not love particularly, but ate because she did not want to offend her new-found hosts. On chicken breasts, sandwiches, lobster, and crisp delicious lettuce. Pre-packed trifle and three sorts of gâteaux. Paul, she noticed, ate sparingly, no second helping of anything. His figure was without a trace of unwanted fat.

'Are you on holiday here, Miss

Dalby?' asked the woman called Anne as she passed Sorelle a glass of champagne.

'No, I work here at the Longchamps Hotel.'

'The one we went to last night,' explained the young man Scott.

'We enjoyed ourselves immensely, Sorelle,' Paul said. 'Nice restaurant you've got there.' He raised his glass. 'A toast to you and your beautiful island.' The others raised theirs but Margot's movement was only perfunctory.

Heat flared in her body again as their eyes locked above the rims. His eyes were chameleon-like, she thought, changing with his moods.

He stood up. 'Who's for a swim?' Then bent over, putting a hand to Sorelle's shoulder, his glance quickly appraising the outline of her upper body moulded against the beach jacket. 'Not you I'm afraid, Sorelle, you've had enough water for today.' His look was faintly mocking.

Sorelle began to rise also. 'You're

right, I've had enough, it's time I was going. You've been very kind and very brave and . . . '

'No — no,' he interrupted, 'you stay here until you've fully recovered.'

She was beginning to notice other things about him, and remembered once seeing an ancient piece of sculpture showing a Roman athlete wrestling with a python. This man reminded her of that magnificent work of art.

The object of her thoughts moved away down the beach followed by the man called Scott.

'I'm coming, Paul,' called Margot, and as she went past Sorelle she muttered, 'Nice try honey, but it won't work.'

Sorelle stared after her angrily. Margot too thought she had done the drowning scene on purpose. Margot was like something out of a magazine, she thought, glossy, everything in place. She wouldn't get out of her depth. Was she married to Paul Melandes? There had not been a ring on her finger. Mistress perhaps? Sorelle felt that it was time to leave.

She found her clothes and bag exactly where she had left them — it seemed a long time since she had entered the water. Thankfully the place by the rock was still unoccupied although the beach was getting busier. She spent a few minutes making herself presentable, then returned the beach jacket to the woman Ann, and thanked her again. Sorelle glanced down the beach on leaving. Paul Melandes, the girl Margot and Scott were still in the water. They didn't see her, had most likely forgotten about her.

Back in her car, Sorelle sank thankfully into the seat, the interior comforting in its warmth and familiarity. She was still somewhat shaken from her experience, but her thoughts were concentrated on the man who had carried her in his arms from the water. Real fear for her had been present in Paul Melandes' eyes when he had been bending over her on the sand after the rescue. And had she so fallen under his spell that her subconscious had in fact taken her deliberately towards his boat?

2

Wednesday morning came. Sorelle, on the early shift, had been very busy with enquiries and interpreting — was often called upon to act in the latter capacity, having a working knowledge of French and German.

She raised her head. Directly opposite across the foyer a man in dark sun-glasses stood watching her. He took them off, a slow smile and a glimpse of white. Paul Melandes. In two swinging strides he was at the desk.

Gleamingly wicked eyes more brown than she had remembered gazed penetratingly into hers. 'Good morning, Miss Sorelle.'

'Morning, Mr Melandes.' She couldn't bring herself to say Paul.

'Paul,' he corrected her sternly. 'You look surprised to see me. I'm here for a few days yet.'

'I — I didn't know how long you would be staying.' She never knew what to say to this man. Always her brain seemed to be paralysed when he was around. 'Are you enjoying your stay?'

'I am and I want you to help me enjoy it even more.' Demons danced in his regard of her.

How did he mean? It was a good thing he could only see the upper part of her — her legs were beginning to tremble.

'When I came out of the water on Sunday you'd gone.'

'Well, I did rather spoil your picnic didn't I?' she said ruefully.

'You're feeling all right now?'

'My thanks to you, yes.'

He looked cool in a lightweight grey jacket and trousers with a white open-neck shirt. His eyebrows, Sorelle observed, had a distinct upward slant to them giving him a roguish look.

'What time d'you finish here?' he asked.

She was faintly surprised at his

directness. 'Three, but by the time I've handed over, it's about quarter past usually.'

'I'll wait for you at the hotel entrance, we'll go somewhere.'

To say that she was taken aback would not adequately describe Sorelle's feelings. And Paul Melandes continued to stare at her in that searching disturbing way that he had, imps of lurking amusement caught by the reception lights.

'Surely I'm not the first man to ask you to meet him?'

She felt a fool but the man penetrated her cool and poise like a rapier. He'd hardly asked her, more like commanded her to meet him. 'Of course not, but I — I did not expect to see you again, and I cannot just leave here and come with you dressed like this.' Sorelle indicated her uniform with a grimace.

He smiled slowly with an expression of knowledgeable insolence. 'You forget I've already seen you in more flattering attire. Remember?'

Indeed she did. On the beach. 'It was you looking at me through the binoculars wasn't it?'

'Yes, it was,' he admitted. 'Beauty by itself is no good. It has to be appreciated by others. The nearest thing to a mermaid I've ever seen.' His eyes grew intent, serious suddenly. 'You were beautiful.'

Then he had carried her in his arms half naked, her flesh against his, though at the time she had been in no fit state to enjoy the sensation. His compliment, however, made her even more agitated. She made an effort to steady herself. Had it just been coincidence that they should both visit that particular bay on the same day?

Just at that moment the telephone rang and people were also approaching the desk; she was going to be busy again.

'I'll be waiting, Sorelle.' His eyes locked on to hers again, then his tall handsome figure was striding away from her.

She was glad when her break came, being unable to concentrate on her work after the visit of Paul Melandes. Had never expected to see him again. And what had happened to Margot, the red-haired woman? Had she been thrown over so soon? Sorelle remembered his arrogance. He had not even asked whether she would like to meet him or not. Taken it for granted that she would. Perhaps he never thought about being refused, a man like that could no doubt have a choice of beautiful women anywhere.

★ ★ ★

Sorelle was excited and a little nervous. Only a few days ago she had envied the woman at Paul's side, now she herself had been asked to accompany him. She looked down at herself — at her work-a-day clothes. How could she meet him in those? And yet she had no time to go home and change.

Paul was waiting for her in a

cherry-red shining Mercedes convertible. He got out, opened the door for her. She blinked in the sunlight after the subdued lighting of the hotel. 'I didn't bring a car of my own over with me, so I hired this for the time being.' He got in, then turned to face her. 'Have you eaten yet?'

'I had a sandwich about twelve-thirty. I usually wait until I get home.' The woody pine smell of his aftershave came to her.

'I've got a few hours, we'll eat somewhere first. All right?'

She smiled her agreement. Anywhere was all right with this man who had suddenly come into her life. If it was a dream she must enjoy it to the full before awakening.

They set off, she guiding him through the small streets away from St. Peter Port. He glanced at her when they had nearly reached the top of the Grange. 'Show me the way to Pleinmont. I rang the Victoria — they sounded efficient.' She knew the Victoria, having been in before — for morning coffee — a nice place.

He drove smoothly along the narrow roads and lanes. Behind the high hedges and past the occasional large greenhouse. Sorelle was enjoying herself. The sun on her face and in the company of an attractive man of the world. She glanced at her companion's profile. Darkly tanned, straight-nosed, and a determined jawline without it being aggressive. His yacht was called the *Privateer*. He too had a piratical look about him.

They reached the coastal road at Cobo Bay, the latter with its sail boarders on the water, and turned to run in sight of the sea to Pleinmont. Sorelle pointed out places of interest to him. Vazon Bay with its wide sweep of sand and fort from the German occupation. The Martello towers dotted along the coast from the Napoleonic Wars, and Lihou Island with its causeway enabling it to be reached at low water.

A corner table overlooking the road

and sea was awaiting them, and Sorelle enjoyed the envious glances thrown in her direction by other women in the restaurant. 'Sandwiches, toast, anything will be all right for me,' she informed him happily.

But Paul called for the full menu.

He looked up from studying it. 'No, it will definitely not be all right for you. I know you have to look after that splendid *petite* figure of yours, but I will not be responsible for the fainting with hunger when you're with me.' He indicated her menu. 'Anything you fancy, you can have it. Now, d'you like sweet or dry white wine? Most women I've known liked it sweet.'

'Then I shall not be the one to break the sequence, Paul, I prefer sweet.' Wondered how many women he had known. Perversely she wished that she had liked dry wine. To be different from the others.

Sorelle had corn-on-the-cob followed by lobster — her favourite with a crisp salad including locally grown tomatoes,

36

followed by pineapple and ginger meringue. She noticed how they had had a waiter to themselves, whilst other customers had to share one with another table. Afterwards she persuaded Paul to share a pot of tea with her.

'Your English ways,' he teased her. Today his eyes reflected the blue-grey sea.

'Guernsey,' she corrected him.

'I thought that the two were the same.' The provocative light was there again.

'No, not quite. We are under the British crown, but we have our own Parliament — the States.'

His eyes probed her face as if noting every feature. 'Are you a native of Guernsey?'

'Yes, but we left the island when I was young,' she told him and proceeded to sketch for him her life since. Then she smiled. 'There, I'm an open book to you.' Something that he was not to her. 'Now you know all about me, it's only fair,' she said with a boldness that surprised herself, 'that you tell me about yourself.'

He leaned forward, elbows on the table, and smiled slowly. It was like the sun sliding from behind grey clouds in the northern town where she used to live. Rare, but appreciated much more when it did occur.

'Washington, Delaware county.'

'The capital. The President lives there doesn't he?' Sorelle aired her knowledge.

'Have you been?'

She smiled wryly. 'No, I haven't been out of Europe. I've seen it on television — that big white building — very impressive.'

Paul clasped his hands together, broad in the palm with strong yet sensitive looking fingers. She noticed the gold ring on the fourth finger. 'I'm Melandes of Melandes fashion shoes and accessories. I'm also the man who podiatrists — chiropodists over here, I believe — held responsible for deforming the feet of half the world's women — young women anyway,' he added with a mischievous gleam.

'I've seen some in the hotel boutique — they're gorgeous. They may not do anything for a girl's feet, but must work wonders for her morale.'

'I could do with you as my press advertising agent, Sorelle,' he chuckled, then went on, 'They sell well and that's all that matters.'

Yes, she thought, that's all that would matter to him. Ruthless in the jungle of business. Her eyes strayed to the patch of dark hair visible in the vee of his shirt. Would he be as ruthless in his private life?

Paul continued, 'I came over to Europe on a business-*cum*-pleasure trip. Keep an eye on how things are progressing over here. Paris, Brussels, Berlin, London — got to call there yet.' His eyes glowed at memories. 'Spent a month in the Med, sure was great. Rome, Nice, shops doing well.'

Suddenly Sorelle was jealous and resentful of the memories that had brought that light to his eyes. Glamorous seductive women no doubt, and of course it would be the same in the places he had yet to visit.

'Am I boring you?' His expression was thoughtful, almost brooding.

'No — no, of course not,' she replied, fastening round blue eyes hastily and attentively on him. They must have strayed with her thoughts. He was from a different world — a world of wealth, high finance, wide flung business interests. A man who made his own decisions, and had the wherewithal and ability to carry them out come what may.

'Then after that, Portugal,' Paul began again.

'Portugal.' Her voice betrayed her special interest.

'You know it?'

'I had a holiday there two years ago — in November. It was beautiful. The Algarve — near Vilamoura.'

His eyes danced into hers. 'Vilamoura! I bought the *Privateer* there.'

Now they had something in
common. Vilamoura. She remembered.
A new lovely marina with magnificant
shops and restaurants, and water
fountains.

'I wondered,' she said, 'when I saw
the name on your boat. Were you in
Portugal on business?'

'No, it was a sentimental journey. My
grandfather came from Faro. He settled
in the States.'

So that was where he got his name
from and his dark handsomeness.

'There,' Paul spread his powerful
hands, 'now you know all about me.'
His gaze held her like a magnet.
Wanted to remain thus as they were
and then to be drawn into his arms.
She took a sip of the lukewarm tea
remaining in her cup, then raised her
head to look at him again. Spoke
hesitantly. 'Paul, did you mistake me
for someone else that day you bumped
into me, and also that night when you

came for dinner at the hotel?'

A narrowing of his eyelids could not hide the sadness which passed swiftly in the depths of his eyes. He nodded. 'You bear a remarkable likeness to someone I knew — on the surface anyway,' then looked away through the window to the sea.

Sorelle heard and guessed at a past bitterness she had invoked in him. 'I'm sorry — I didn't mean to pry or . . . '

'You didn't,' he interjected, 'it wasn't anything — never was anything.'

She could only guess at the cause of that bitterness — a woman obviously. A broken love affair?

Paul beckoned the waiter, paid the bill. He seemed restless suddenly as if her question had awakened other disturbing thoughts in him. Standing up he came around the table, leaned over her, she was conscious of his male body warmth as he held her chair away for her, then gently placed his hand on her waist and led her from the restaurant.

The passenger seat was hot to her back through her blouse. Paul looked at her, his hand on the ignition key. The serious look of a minute ago had gone — a challenging one had replaced it. 'I'm going to let the car go where it will. You tell me where we are and what's what. You're the courier on this trip.'

They set off going inland again along the sunlit, sometimes shaded lovely lanes. Past the old underground hospital. She showed him the little chapel, one of the smallest in the world, made mostly of Ormer shells. Past contented cows in the small fields, tiny woods, then pointed out the house where she was born.

He stopped the car, gazed at the house, then at the calm and green countryside around them. Shook his head in wonder. 'It's so fresh, so much beauty in a small area.' His eyes came to rest on Sorelle. 'That's something that I could attribute to you also.' His look slipped from her face to her shoulders, caressed her body slowly with a practised arrogance.

A pulsating warmth flowed through her as his gaze returned to her face. She glanced away pretending to look at something, and was relieved when they moved off again, and glad that he did not speak for a while. He had paid her a nice compliment, but no doubt he was experienced at doing that — she shouldn't read too much into it. Just a meal and an afternoon drive. He had mentioned having only a few hours free, and she wondered what he was going to do when they parted.

'Where are we now, Sorelle?' His voice startled her from her thoughts.

'Hauteville. This is Hauteville.' A narrow street of terraced nineteenth-century houses, guest houses and small shops — one of the older parts of St Peter Port. She pointed at a building on the right. 'That's Victor Hugo's house.'

'The writer?' She was surprised at his show of interest.

'Yes, he was exiled here in Guernsey. Want to go in?'

Paul had already stopped the car. 'Well, being a businessman I like to see the other side of the coin. People who have created. Writers, artists, those people. See how they live, and where. But you'll have seen it before?'

She shrugged, smiled. 'I don't mind — it's an interesting place.'

'You're my guide this afternoon you know.' His smile lit up his face and her heart at the same time, as they entered the tall terraced building.

It was gloomy inside after the sunlit street. She had always found it rather a forbidding house. It wasn't busy and after Paul had paid, the guide came forward to take them around. Paul drew her aside and murmured something, the woman's face coming to life with an understanding smile.

He took Sorelle's arm as they began their tour of the house alone. 'But I thought you had to have a guide; there's always been one when I've come before,' Sorelle told him puzzled. 'What did you say to her?'

'That we were on our honeymoon — married yesterday.' Paul stopped and looked down into her face, his own in the shadows so that she could not see its expression. 'And that we were just getting used to being alone together.'

Sorelle could not help catching her breath at the thrill the words gave her. If only what he had told the woman were true. But his voice had held a cynical hard amusement, as if he could never envisage marriage to anyone.

They inspected the lower rooms, or rather Paul did. Sorelle was too busy watching her companion. A modern man in an old house, she thought, yet something of its strength about him — tall, his musculature hard like the wood carving abounding everywhere. Going upstairs she was conscious of his thigh touching against hers. Past the tapestries covering the walls, then up another flight of narrower stairs to the attic-like place where the writer used to work.

Halfway up Sorelle determined to find out about something which had been puzzling her. 'Paul, did you know that I would be at Moulin Huet last Sunday?'

They paused on the steps and he looked back down at her. 'Of course I did. I don't leave that sort of thing to chance.' His tone was self-assured, confident.

'But I didn't tell anyone as far as I remember,' Sorelle said, even more puzzled.

'I just asked that's all.' She saw his teeth gleam in the sombre light of the stairs. 'The head waiter told me that it was ninety per cent certain that if your day off fell on a Sunday it would be Moulin Huet you'd go to.'

Sorelle's heart leapt. So he had been interested enough to take his yacht to Moulin Huet to find her.

'You were easy to find; you were the only one with half a swim suit. It didn't take me long to spot you through the glasses.'

Sorelle flushed. At the top of the stairs she fought to keep her voice steady as she pointed out the two ledges that the great writer used, with the old stove between them. 'When he got tired of writing on one, he moved across to the other,' she explained.

They stood looking out through the window to the islands of Sark and Herm, with Jersey and the faint outline of the French coast beyond, Castle Cornet in the near distance. Sounds from the town were muted.

Down below was the rose garden and conservatory. She could see people walking about in it. 'Did you know, Paul, that the Guernsey rose is supposed to be the finest in the world? I heard that on the radio the other day.' She glanced round at him to find him observing her.

He reached out, touched her cheeks in turn lightly with the back of his fingers. 'You have roses in your English cheeks.'

Her body quivered momentarily at

the exquisite pleasure of his touch. 'Guernsey roses,' she corrected him throatily.

'Beautiful whichever they are.' His voice was deep, husky suddenly.

She was in a tunnel, his face blotting out everything else. It was hot, very hot. A sudden happiness had welled up inside her, nearly choking her. She wished the afternoon would last for ever.

His fingers left her face to lightly caress her shoulders. Then without speaking he gently took hold of her hand and led her towards the stairs again. It was just as well, she thought, though slightly disappointed that he had not kissed her. She would have had little defence if he had decided there and then to add her to his list of conquests.

Hand in his she followed him as they descended the stairs. Halfway down her heel caught in the stair edge. She stumbled. Paul turned swiftly breaking her fall. Her free hand clutched round his neck to steady herself, she coming to a halt safely in his arms against the full length of his lean body. Very close, feeling the rock-like hardness of his thighs pressed against hers. Just for a moment Sorelle dangled from him like the prey of a hunter. Then his strong arms moved to her waist and lifted her back on to the step above. Even so, he still towered over her.

Her heart seemed to have deserted its usual place and was fluttering like a caged bird inside her. The light from the room they had just left shone down dimly on Paul's face. His hands did not leave her waist. When she looked up at him his eyes held hers with a startling intensity which encompassed her, conscious of the overwhelming magnetic charge between them. His lips descended devouringly on hers with a thrusting force. A mad excitement stirred then rippled through her being. What will she had left told her to withdraw — get away from him. But she was helpless, her traitorous lips seeking his, her body responding to forces stronger than her mind. Their hearts were as one, pounding against each other's body.

Sorelle felt that her legs would no longer support her — did not seem to belong to her any more. Her whole being was becoming limp under the assault her senses were receiving from his dominating mouth. Drawn further and further into an abyss of pure pleasure. Even when the pressure of his lips softened on hers, she was reluctant to allow them to withdraw. To her chagrin she was aware of this even as their kiss ended and ashamed that he had stirred so strong a feeling in her on such short acquaintance.

She was glad of the gloom in the staircase. Paul would not see her features clearly. Her lips were level with the dark hairs visible above his open shirt as she croaked breathlessly, 'M — my shoe caught in the steps.' It sounded stupid, she knew it did. A person could stumble without ending up locked in a passionate embrace in the arms of a man she had known only a short time.

Paul drew away so that he could look at her. The animal light was receding slowly from his eyes, and he must have caught the sound of an apology in her utterance. 'My, my, I wouldn't have missed that for anything,' he said boldly and huskily. The palms of his strong hands were still across her waist. Could feel their warmth through the top of her skirt.

Her face flushed in shame. He knew the reaction that he had so easily aroused in her. At that moment she disliked herself. Paul's hand found one of hers and helped her down the remaining stairs with, she thought, exaggerated care. She was glad to be on the move again, it giving her time to calm and compose herself.

He halted on the landing before they descended the next flight to the ground floor. The sunlight through an open bedroom door illuminated him like a picture with a light over it. The sort of face that would look good under a gladiator's helmet. Smiling wryly he said, 'It's a good thing you're not wearing a pair of Melandes shoes, I should never have heard the last of it.'

It was highly unlikely that she would have been wearing a pair of those — they were not for a girl on a receptionist's salary.

Paul began to lead her down to the hallway. Spoke over his shoulder in humorous tones. 'You know, Sorelle, it seems to me that you do an awful lot of stumbling. You have the walk of a gazelle, and any man could watch you move for hours, and yet ... ' He glanced back at her and she glimpsed the mocking glint, 'you stumbled into me by the harbour, stumbled in the water last Sunday, and now you fall into my arms in this house today. If Monsieur Hugo is watching, I'll bet the *Privateer* that he's got a whole lot of twinkle in his eye.'

Sorelle meant to respond, to match

his mood, but instead she said stiffly, 'I did not stumble into you on the harbour walk. If you remember you bumped into me after you climbed up the steps from your yacht.'

'So I did, I'd forgotten.' He was laughing at her, she knew.

She decided she must try and be a little more gracious, soften somewhat. 'Well,' she admitted, 'I suppose if you hadn't been there to catch me each time I should have been out of this world or at the very least have hurt myself.'

He glanced sideways at her with a shameless gleam as they went along the hall. 'You're a very catchable woman, Sorelle, I don't mind at all.' She wondered how he could be so relaxed and cool whilst her whole being was still tingling from their kiss upon the stairs.

Outside his regard of her altered, some concern showing. 'Are you all right? You didn't hurt yourself on the stairs?'

'No.' She thanked him with her eyes.

'Just the shock, that's all,' thinking to herself that her body had received two shocks, one unpleasant, the other very pleasant indeed. Nevertheless, he helped her into her seat, his powerful but gentle hands on her upper arms, his mouth just brushing her hair as he bent over her.

They threaded their way through the town traffic again and she wondered where they were going, remembering that he had said they would only have a few hours together. As if he had read her thoughts he glanced at her, 'We're sailing in about another hour, so . . . '

'Sailing?' She couldn't help her interruption. Hoped that her surprise and disappointment would not be too evident in her voice.

'Yes, I have to go.'

As he stopped the car outside her flat she said with a light-heartedness of manner she did not feel, 'Well, this is it. This is where I live.' The prospect of the evening alone — an anticlimax after the stimulating company of the attractive man behind the wheel.

He turned in his seat to face her. 'Thanks for being my guide, Sorelle. It's been great — I've enjoyed everything.'

She heard the emphasis on everything. Did his eyes now have more grey than brown in them? 'And thank you, Paul. I've enjoyed it immensely — such a lovely surprise. Usually I just leave work — the days are very much alike . . . ' She hesitated awkwardly — knew she sounded stilted. But could she have been anything else? Half an hour ago she had been welded to this man in the most passionate kiss she had ever experienced, her whole body crying out, lost in his arms. Now in the sunlight a formal goodbye. She made to get out of the car.

Paul came round, opened the door for her, then got straight back into his seat again. A glance over his shoulder at the traffic, a wave of his hand to her and he was gone. He did not look back or wave again, and she turned and let herself into her flat, feeling strangely miserable and deflated.

Had their kiss meant so little to him that he could just go off like that? Probably he had thought her easy and cheap the way she had responded so strongly in his embrace. Began to wish she had never taken him to the Maison Hugo. What did it matter now? She would probably never see Paul Melandes again. For an afternoon she had been Cinderella with her prince. Now the coach had gone taking him with it. Not all fairy-tales had a happy ending.

3

The next day was her day off. Usually she looked forward to this break, but she could not settle to anything. In the evening she went to the theatre at the new leisure centre. But try as she might to ignore it, the face of Paul Melandes invariably came between herself and those on the stage.

It was with some relief that she settled into her chair behind her desk at the hotel the next morning. Welcomed the fact that, it being Friday, it would be busy and keep her thoughts from straying. About eleven o'clock when she had just finished giving room keys to new guests, the telephone rang. Her assistant Stella took the call.

'For you, Miss Dalby, from the *Privateer*.' She looked puzzled. 'Is that a hotel?'

Sorelle's heart had begun to race as

soon as she heard the yacht's name. Didn't explain, took the phone.

A woman's voice — American. 'Miss Dalby? Sorelle Dalby? Have I got the right person?'

'Yes, Miss Dalby speaking.'

'Oh, good. This is Ann from the *Privateer*.'

Ann? 'Perhaps you've forgotten — we met on the beach.'

Sorelle remembered the dark-haired woman in Paul Melandes' beach party. Wondered what she wanted. 'Yes, of course I remember, you gave me your jacket. It was kind and helpful of you.'

'You were welcome — so long as you're feeling better now.'

'I'm fine thanks.' She was still puzzled.

'Oh good. Well, Mr Melandes is throwing a cocktail party on Saturday night — tomorrow, nine o'clock. He'd like you to be there. He's busy right now, but asked me to contact you.'

For a few moments Sorelle struggled to get over her surprise.

'Hello.'

'Y — yes, — er — thank you, Ann.'

'Can you manage it? Will you be free?'

'Yes, I'll be there.' Her quickened breathing must be audible to the woman on the other end.

'For Pete's sake don't forget.' A trace of anxiety had entered the other's voice. 'There'd be hell to pay if he thought I hadn't contacted you. When Mr Paul Melandes wants something he generally gets it.'

Yes, I'm sure he does, thought Sorelle.

'You'll know the Albert Marina,' went on Ann, 'Well, we're anchored behind it in the outer harbour. If you come along the pier, a boat will be waiting to bring you over. OK?'

Sorelle knew where she meant. 'Yes, I'll be ready, but I don't know what I'm going to wear though,' she confessed.

'Don't worry, honey, you'll find something. You'll look great,' said Ann encouragingly. 'See you Saturday.'

'Oh, Ann.'

'Yes.'

'Thank Paul — Mr Melandes for the invitation — very kind of him.'

'I will Sorelle, honey.' She rang off.

Had there been a faint note of cynicism? Sorelle put the receiver down, an excited astonishment filling her. She leaned against the desk.

Stella was looking at her with a concerned curiosity. 'Are you all right? Not bad news?'

Sorelle glanced at her, shook her head vigorously. 'It certainly isn't. It's the best news I've had for a while, that's for sure.'

For the remainder of the day her mind was busy with thoughts of the coming cocktail party on board the yacht *Privateer*.

She was excited at the prospect of meeting again the most attractive and magnetic man she had ever known, and also already a little nervous. What could she wear? What had she for an occasion like that? And her hair, it was too late for an appointment that day, and tomorrow was Saturday when she wouldn't finish until three again. Perhaps Marie in the hotel salon would push her in. Sorelle sighed, it was all at such short notice. She felt a sudden irritation with Paul Melandes. Just like him to expect everybody to jump to do his bidding.

On leaving work she drove home more quickly than usual. Once inside she went straight into her bedroom and flung open the wardrobe door, surveyed the assorted clothes hanging there with a sense of hopelessness.

Then the thought came. What harm would there be in just having a look into the hotel boutique? They may just have something inexpensive that she could wear to the party. If she was going to meet Paul Melandes again she must look her very best.

During her morning break she paid a visit to Patti at the boutique, but one glance at the prices on the tickets made her heart sink.

Patti was determined to help. 'A cocktail party you said. I think I've something that's just made for you here.' She threw an envious glance at Sorelle's figure then pulled a dress off one of the rails, spread it over her hands.

Sorelle drew in her breath — the garment was beautiful. Then saw the price — more than twice what she could really afford. 'I'm sorry, Patti, it's just too much. I should have known. Sorry to have you . . . '

'Look,' interrupted Patti, 'do you want it?'

Sorelle's face gave its answer. 'All right then, half down this week, half next. How's that?'

'You're a marvel, Patti, I'll call for it later,' then hurried back to reception.

Sat in the hairdressing salon after finishing work Sorelle felt the tension and excitement mounting in her. Marie looked at her through the mirror. 'I could tell by your voice this morning, somebody special?'

'Yes, he's very special. To tell you the truth, Marie, I never thought I'd see him again.'

'In that case we'd better make sure that you look great and then you'll keep him.' Her fingers moved expertly, until Sorelle's golden hair was done in the fashionable Princess Diana style. As she was leaving, Marie said to her, 'I hope this man appreciates what you're doing for him.'

'So do I, Marie,' she echoed fervently. The other gazed after her. Hoped she would not get hurt, having heard that it was a wealthy older man.

Once home Sorelle had a bath and afterwards nibbled at a sandwich. She wasn't really hungry, butterflies beginning to flutter in her stomach. At seven o'clock she began to dress for the evening and when she had finished she surveyed herself critically in the mirror.

The new dress was mini-length to just above the knee in a brown soft jersey material which clung to and outlined her feminine curves. The collar and a broad vee down the front pointing at the waist was in contrasting white. A narrow gold chain encircled her waist. She wore dark gold high-heeled sandals, the colour almost matching the golden tan of her bare legs. Over her shoulders she slung her white blazer jacket. It could be cool by the water. In her hand she carried a small brown clutch bag.

At ten minutes to nine she was turning on to the pier.

After parking her car she strolled towards the end wall of the pier and looked across the outer harbour. A white yacht which she immediately recognised as the *Privateer* lay some two hundred yards away and dressed from stem to stern with coloured lights. The water was so calm that it was as if the boat was a model placed upon a mirror. A small boat lay to a boarding ladder at the yacht's side and Sorelle saw people moving about on deck.

As she continued to watch, the small boat detached itself from the *Privateer* and headed in the direction of the pier. She made her way down the steps to the landing-stage to be ready, pulling her jacket around her — it being cooler under the pier.

The boat's engine throttled back as it slid gently in alongside where she stood, the disturbed water lapping gently at the stonework. A middle-aged brown faced man in a white jacket and cap stood up in the stern and handed her in, after ascertaining in a pronounced accent that she was a guest of Mr Melandes, then motioned her into the cabin. Sorelle thanked him, sure that she had glimpsed a twinkle in his glance as she stepped aboard. The cabin was small but cosy with a red velvet seat down each side. It was obvious that she was the only passenger on that trip and felt quite important. No doubt there would be more guests arriving later as it was early yet.

Sorelle climbed the yacht's boarding ladder, her breathing becoming shallow and not all because of the exertion.

Aware of faces above her, gazing over the side. Music was coming from somewhere. She stepped aboard, then hesitated, glanced about her.

Paul Melandes detached himself from a couple nearby and came forward to greet her. He must have been watching for her. Her heart leapt at his approach. He wore a white lightweight suit with short sleeves, his tanned hairy muscular arms appearing darker by contrast. His eyes slid over her admiringly. 'Welcome aboard the *Privateer*, Sorelle, great of you to come.' Raised her hand to his lips. His expression raised her confidence, the touch of his lips burning a sensual thrill through her.

'It was nice of you to ask me, Paul.' It had been more like a command, she remembered.

'You look beautiful,' he murmured. She began to lose herself in his eyes.

'Come and meet some of the others,' and hand on her lower waist he guided her through the open glass doors into the saloon. It was already crowded, warm, the music she had heard coming from the far corner — she glimpsed the pianist. Paul took her to a group near the centre of the room. Sorelle recognised them as being the people she had met on the beach — only the girl Margot was missing.

He introduced them again. Maurice and his wife Ann, and Scott the fair-haired younger man, then smilingly remarked, 'Rather different circumstances from the last time you met them, Sorelle.'

'Please don't remind me,' she laughed with a shudder. Felt pleased at the admiring looks the two men had given her, and the one of approval from Ann.

Paul addressed the others, 'I told her that if she wished to inspect my yacht, this was the best way to do it.' He focused on her again, his words making her feel slightly uncomfortable. Was he inferring again that she had attracted his attention deliberately in the water that day?

Just then a steward appeared at his elbow with some message. Paul turned to them, 'More guests — I must see them aboard, please excuse me.' His eyes danced into Sorelle's. 'Look after this delightful creature for me, don't let her get away,' and then he left them, his broad-shouldered narrow-hipped back disappearing on to the after deck.

The woman Ann raised her eyebrows at Sorelle. 'You're obviously the one in favour right now, Sorelle.'

Yes, for now, the latter thought. That's how the game was played. Shield your heart and you'd be all right. 'I suppose so, Ann,' she agreed with a light-heartedness she did not altogether feel.

For a while the four of them chatted, they telling her how much they liked Guernsey, and St Peter Port in particular. 'I'd say,' Scott opined, 'one of the most beautiful harbours in the world. The place is beginning to grow on me.' He smiled and she thought he had a nice one — boyish and open.

'And unspoilt,' added Maurice.

Sorelle expressed her pleasure at their praise of her island but then was surprised to learn that they had been to Jersey also.

'Yeah. We've just spent three days there, Sorelle,' Scott informed her. So that was where Paul had been going last Wednesday.

Ann was regarding her husband affectionately. 'Maurice, do I remember Paul asking you and Scott to circulate!'

'I guess you did Ann, sweet. We'd better do just that eh, Scott. I think the women want to talk woman talk.'

His wife smiled. 'I don't want you looking for another job at your age.'

Maurice laughed, no way perturbed at the suggestion, then he and Scott excused themselves to Sorelle and moved away amongst the other guests.

'Is Mr Melandes such a slave driver,' she asked.

'Well, he's a go-getter — always has been. If there's business about, he wants a share of it.' Ann paused then said, 'I'm glad you made it tonight.' She seemed pleased to have Sorelle to talk to, was vibrant-faced, elfin-like with urchin-cropped dark hair in a red trouser suit. 'Does your husband work for Mr Melandes?' enquired Sorelle.

'Yes, he's one of Paul's senior executives — he manages the European scene.'

'And that young man, Scott, does he work for him also?'

Ann nodded. 'Yes, he's our representative in Hong Kong. He's done well, so has Maurice. This is Paul's way of saying thank you. Every year he takes senior staff on a holiday-*cum*-business trip.'

So he had a kindly streak beneath his business ruthlessness, thought Sorelle.

'Maurice,' went on Ann, 'has been with Paul almost from the beginning — I guess about twelve years now, soon after the break-up.'

'Break-up?' queried Sorelle intrigued.

Ann's voice became a whisper, moved her head closer. 'If Paul knew I was telling you this he'd have me thrown over the side.'

Sorelle shook her head. 'I won't say anything, Ann.' She was deeply curious to know more about him.

'Well it seems that when Paul was about twenty he fell in love with a girl — completely in love with her. More intense on his side than on hers I believe. He wasn't wealthy then, but he had a job. She said she'd marry him.'

Ann continued with a sympathetic frown, 'Then it seems right at the last minute — the day of the wedding — she called it off. Went and married some man loaded with money.' She took a sip of her drink, then regarded Sorelle thoughtfully. 'The day we docked, Paul bumped into you on the quay side didn't he?'

'He certainly did,' said Sorelle decisively; she hadn't forgotten the incident, nor would she ever.

'It gave him a shock, because he told Maurice afterwards that you looked very much like the girl who'd deserted him. He knew you couldn't be of course, but all the same . . . '

So that was it, Sorelle realised, the fleeting memory of a past hurt brought on by her likeness to that girl he had intended to marry.

Trying to keep her tone casual, she asked. 'And is Paul married now?'

Ann laughed shortly, cynically, surprise evident in her expression at the question. 'Is he married? You're kidding, Sorelle honey. He's the man most likely to remain unmarried in the whole wide world, that's for sure.' Her gaze suddenly sharpened on the younger woman. 'Don't get me wrong though, he's a man — you'll have guessed that by now.'

She certainly had. 'Is he a woman-hater then?' Sorelle was puzzled. From her short acquaintance with Paul, he had not appeared to be that sort otherwise why should she be there on his invitation?

'Oh no, he likes women.' Her look became meaningful. 'He loves them

— one after the other.'

For a moment Sorelle felt revulsion at Ann's disclosures, but what had she expected a man like Paul Melandes to be like? Such a handsome, vital, sexual man — of course he would have sought and taken his pleasure whenever he wanted. In some peculiar fashion she had placed him on a pedestal, making him a celibate man saving himself for the right girl — herself? 'Maybe it's because he was jilted like that,' she suggested.

'I think it's certainly coloured his attitude to our sex,' nodded Ann. She emptied her glass but still held it and shot a glance at Sorelle. 'Any woman who thinks she hears wedding bells with him is on to a loser. Have a good time while it lasts, but that's all, honey.'

It sounded like a direct warning for her own good, thought Sorelle. Well, now she knew.

Glancing through the large windows of the yacht, she saw that it was almost dark outside with lights twinkling in the distance. Above the conversations and tinkling of glasses the pianist was playing 'Misty'. It made her want to dance to the beautiful melody, and preferably with the man who had invited her on board that evening. Turning back to Ann she asked, 'Where is your friend, Margot, is she here?' and hoping that the red-headed woman would not be.

'She's somewhere about, probably eyeing the talent coming aboard,' was Ann's frank and matter-of-fact reply.

So Paul could not mean so much to her, nor she to him for that matter, thought Sorelle. 'What does she do? Is she one of his employees?'

Ann wrinkled her forehead. 'Well, not really an employee. Margot's extremely wealthy. Married an older man. When he died he left her everything.'

Sorelle was puzzled. Ann saw it. 'She's a great designer of women's shoes, and accessories. Comes out with some staggering styles. That's why he tolerates her, she's good for the

75

business.' Sorelle's companion paused then added, 'But I think they've a lot in common.'

'Oh.' Sorelle could not keep the curiosity out of her voice.

'Yes, they're both collectors.'

'Collectors?' Ann would think she was simple and naïve. What on earth did she mean?

The other's face expressed a faint surprise. 'Sorry, honey, perhaps you call them something else. He collects ladies' hearts — she collects the men's — they're hunters. A conquest a day keeps the doctor away.' She laughed wryly at her attempted joke. 'Hell, Sorelle, you know what I mean.' Yes, she certainly did understand — now. Ann hadn't finished. 'It was rumoured that she'd asked him to marry her. I don't think she meant anything to him but for once I think he did to her.' Ann smiled at some memory. 'Poor Margot. She sulked and stayed away for about three months, but she came round in the end.'

Sorelle was glad Margot had not got her own way. Just at that moment she saw Paul returning with more guests. Margot was with him. He then made his way towards herself and Ann with Margot holding on to his arm possessively. Sorelle had to admit that Margot looked stunning. Copper hair in frizzy curls framing her face, and wearing a black calf-length dress with three parallel bands of green lace across the bodice. A four-string loop of huge pearls swung from her neck. Her green eyes swept with cold impatient disdain over Sorelle, the latter suddenly feeling both ill dressed and groomed by comparison.

Even though Ann had told her that there was nothing between them, a stab of intense jealousy went through her at the sight of Margot on his arm. She wondered if Margot had known she was attending.

'Deserted by the men,' said Paul with a bantering concern.

'They're mingling,' Ann told him.

He glanced at their hands. 'What's this? Empty glasses on the *Privateer*?'

'I'm staying dry this round, Paul,' said Ann.

He looked down on Sorelle from his great height. 'I'm going to get you the *Privateer* cocktail.'

'*Privateer* cocktail?'

He nodded, smiling. 'The yacht's own special cocktail — special to the *Privateer*. Try it?' His eyes challenged hers. They had darkened in the artificial light, and behind them she was aware of a passionate desire reaching out to her.

The effect was to make her voice tremulous. 'Is it very strong?'

'Very potent.' The words and his deep voice which had softened perceptibly stroked her sensually.

Her vivid blue eyes laughed into his. 'Then I'll try one, Paul.' She must sound like a fool — unworldly. He must think her very unsophisticated. But she was pleased and flattered at his attention to her in front of Margot. That person's cat's eyes were, she noticed, beginning to wander. Paul left her and went to get the cocktail — going for it himself, Sorelle noted.

For the few minutes that he was gone Ann and Margot chatted, the latter completely ignoring Sorelle. But Sorelle noticed that even as Margot was talking her eyes were restlessly surveying the room, or rather, Sorelle guessed, the men in it. She couldn't have Paul, was jealous of another woman having his attentions, yet she herself was not averse to affairs with other men if Ann was to be believed.

The cocktail was unlike any other alcoholic drink she had ever tasted. 'It's got rum, ginger wine, vodka, pineapple,' Paul explained, then added mysteriously, a glitter in his eyes as they pinned hers, 'and one or two other things.' Sorelle felt the pick up of her heart beats immediately. This man she realised had the ability to play upon her physical and mental emotions at will. There was a touch of satisfied arrogance as he turned from her in answer to Margot's irritable clutch at his arm.

Soon afterwards the buffet was announced, and Sorelle with the others went down the short flight of stairs into the main state room. A large polished wood-panelled room with tables on three sides piled high with a wide variety of food. As she moved along putting tasty things upon her plate, Sorelle heard Paul's unmistakable voice at her ear. 'Can I get you anything?'

He was so close that if she had turned a little more, their mouths would have met. Thoughts of the food almost disappeared. 'I seem to be doing very well thanks, Paul.'

'Are you enjoying yourself?'

'I certainly am.' Her eyes shone into his. 'And thank you very much for asking me here tonight.' She noticed he had a half filled glass in his hand. 'You're not eating?'

He gave a tiny shake of his head, a twinkle in his eyes. 'I'm leaving that to my guests.'

Her eyes caught sight of a plateful of

Guernsey *gâche* — a fruit loaf spread with butter. Sorelle was pleased to see it, though it was such ordinary fare amongst some of the other more exotic food present. 'Look Paul, take some of that Guernsey *gâche*, it's an island speciality' — a simple obvious thing. Was it like her — an island girl, simple and obvious.

'Looks interesting,' he murmured but didn't take any. She spotted some ormers — shell fish. 'Try one of those Paul. They're nice — caught round the islands.'

'Perhaps I will,' he spoke in her ear lazily, 'but you know something.' She turned to look questioningly at him, 'I'm beginning to think that you must teach me more about this island of yours.' Then he left her and she began to move along on limbs that had in the last few minutes become surprisingly weak.

Later she freshened herself up in the ladies' room, looked at her flushed bright-eyed face. Smoothed her dress

— it didn't look too bad after all. At first she had thought she was out of place wearing a short dress amongst the long evening gowns worn by some but a few more had arrived wearing minis.

In the saloon again she saw Paul was busily engaged in close conversation with two other men. Maurice was talking to another couple whilst Scott was listening attentively to a young woman. Of Ann there was no sign. The pianist was playing one of the latest songs of the American singer Barry Manilow. Then champagne was served and Sorelle picked the glass with the smallest amount in it.

She wandered out on the after deck. A few couples were dancing, others embracing in the shadows and some individuals leaning over the yacht's rail. She stood looking out over the water seeing the masts of other yachts outlined in the inner harbour. The well-lit esplanade, the moving head-lights of cars and the kaleidoscope of colours from the buildings rising up from the town. Heard the chimes of the church clock floating across. And overheard the dark warm vault of the summer sky.

Sorelle watched as the night ferry to the mainland began to slip away from White Rock jetty. For some passengers the last glimpse of the island — holidays over. Had some found romance? Would her romance in the shape of Paul Melandes slip away one night in the *Privateer*, to become just a memory?

'Ah, there you are all by yourself? Always when I look for you — you seem to have a habit of vanishing.' His voice made her start; it was almost as if he had known her thoughts.

'I — I was just enjoying the view. I saw you were in conversation so I came out here, it's such a lovely night.' The lights hanging above had recoloured his white suit, and bathed her face in a dark red glow.

'I think it will be lovelier when you dance with me,' he murmured, drawing her into his arms. They began to sway to the slow rhythm of the music coming clearly from the saloon, only the lightweight cloth of his suit and her thin dress separating them. She was aware of the hardness of his chest against her cheek and the warmth from him.

With an effort she lifted her head, said hesitantly, 'I thought that — that you were with . . . '

'Margot,' he finished for her. 'Oh she's about somewhere, enjoying herself no doubt.' His tone was careless, dismissive, and Sorelle was surprised. It was different when he spoke again — huskily, admiringly. 'You look beautiful, Sorelle and it's a great dress you're wearing. Is it new?'

'Yes, I bought it for tonight, well half bought it anyway.' She gave a wry smile then immediately regretted telling him — had no idea why she had, it had just slipped out. He did not comment on her remark, but brought her hard against himself again, his lips caressing her hair.

'The women have been casting envious looks at you all night,' he whispered. 'As for the men, it's a good thing you're now safe in my arms. I imagine there'll be one or two divorces after tonight.'

Sorelle sighed happily. It was nice to have compliments paid like that, even though they came from the lips of a man well practised no doubt in the art. The music stopped and she remained for the moment in his embrace, not really wanting to leave it. She heard the church clock striking again. Wondered hazily what time it was. She had been under a spell — a powerful spell cast by the man holding her. Drew away from him slowly, 'I shall have to be going soon, Paul. I'm sorry but I have to be up early in the morning.' The thought brought her nearer to reality.

'What, so soon?' His eyes were very dark, drugged like. He let her go reluctantly. 'I'm sure you won't be turned into a pumpkin if you don't get home before midnight.' There was a mockery and disappointment in his voice.

'No,' she sighed, 'but perhaps the next worse thing — I might lose my job.'

Paul took her hand. 'I've been meaning to talk to you about that. Have a coffee before you go.' He began to lead her gently towards the saloon. That would be nice before she went home. But what did he mean about her job? She glanced back over the yacht's rail. The ferry was just an oblong of yellow lights out at sea. She was a Cinderella — had met her Prince, and now it was the end of the ball. Soon it would be her turn to leave also.

They sat together in the state room over their coffee. Sorelle felt that she had enjoyed herself. The man by her side had paid a lot of attention to her considering that he had many people aboard his yacht.

'What are you thinking about?' His eyes were fixed on her, observing her closely. She shrugged. 'Oh, just that all this will seem like a dream when I'm behind the desk in the morning.'

'We can soon alter that, Sorelle. I want you to come and work for me.'

'Work for you!' she exclaimed in astonishment, her cup halted halfway to her lips. 'But I — I . . . ' She couldn't find words. What an unpredictable man this was, watching her with an amused gleam. She recovered enough to begin again. 'W — what as? What work could I do for you?'

'I want you to model for me. Shoes, accessories, maybe clothes, everything.'

She stared at him wide-eyed, gave a quick confused shake of her head. 'But where? Where would I have to go?'

'Oh,' he opened his hands, shrugged slightly, a half smile appearing, 'the States, Europe, London — you name the place.'

'Are you serious?' Her eyes devoured his face searching for some sign that he was not.

His eyes fell to her lips, held a desire. 'I've never been more serious,' he stated simply. 'Think it over — let me know tomorrow.'

'Tomorrow!' Her mind was in a whirl. At getting on for one o'clock in the morning she couldn't begin to think of making a decision like that. 'But I'd have to give a month's notice anyway.' Sorelle couldn't think of anything else to say at that moment.

'Why would you have to do that?' His tone suggested that she was a child bothering him with some minor problem.

'Because I could lose a month's salary if I did not.'

'Huh, don't worry about that.' Paul dismissed her anxiety with a wave of his hand. 'I'll make that up for you before you start. As an employee of Melandes Incorporated you'll earn plenty, I'll see to that.'

The word employee sobered her from her earlier romantic thoughts. It sounded cold and impersonal. But that's what she would be — an employee. 'But I've never done any modelling,' she pointed out.

'You've got everything it takes, Sorelle.' His eyes became hooded, desire flickering in them. 'Don't forget I've seen you pretty well all over.'

Sorelle felt her face beginning to colour. His voice had held overtones of ownership. Powerfully magnetic and charming he was, but she was coming to realise that he was egotistical and domineering also. She knew she must be going, being at once tired, excited and confused. Wanted to be alone now and think Paul's surprising offer over.

He draped her coat over her shoulders, his fingers touching her causing a tremor to run through her. 'Did you bring your car into the town, Sorelle?'

'It's at the end of the jetty, quite close to the steps.'

'Leave it there. I'll have someone pick it up in the morning and delivered to your flat,' Paul ordered. 'A cab will take you home.'

'A cab,' she exclaimed surprised. 'It's kind of you Paul and thanks, but the car is there.'

'Yes, and it will stay there,' he said sternly with a slight up-turning of his mouth corners belying his tone. 'I've had a cab on call for you since midnight.' She rose and offered her grateful thanks. No doubt about it, he certainly got things done.

Arm around her waist he began to lead her towards the after deck. She looked back to say goodbye to the others. Could only see Ann and Maurice. Caught their eyes — they waved. Some couples were still dancing outside. When she and Paul had nearly reached the boarding steps, he pulled her gently back by the hands towards him, into the shadows away from the lights.

She looked up at him from her medium height and smiled, 'Thanks for a gorgeous evening — for everything Paul.'

'You're very welcome, Sorelle,' he uttered with a deep huskiness. 'I'll see you tomorrow.'

'Tomorrow?'

'Yes, then you can tell me you're going to work for me.' She couldn't help smiling at his supreme confidence. 'I'll call for you at three fifteen again.'

She nodded bemused but then remembered. 'I can't, I'm working the late shift.'

'All right, be ready at say eleven. We'll go for a walk, have lunch somewhere and I'll have you back in time.' He glanced towards the town. 'I think I ought to come to the jetty with you,' he said with some concern.

'No, I shall be all right,' she assured him. 'Anyway you still have guests to look after.'

'More's the pity,' he sighed. He lifted her right hand to his lips, caressed the backs of her fingers. The sensation caused her to draw in her breath quickly. The sound was soft, barely audible, yet it must have triggered off something in Paul. In a moment her mouth and body were being crushed in his arms. But then abruptly he let go, and with a movement of great strength placed her bodily away from him. He leaned over the side, called out, 'Carlos. Miss Dalby is ready to be taken back to the jetty.'

Sorelle went down the steps weak-legged and her emotions in a whirl. She glanced upwards after stepping into the boat, but Paul had gone.

By the time she was in the taxi she had brought some sort of order to her thoughts. How marvellous it would be to work for him, see the places that he had mentioned where she would work. She dreamed of seeing herself on the catwalks of fashion shows throughout the world, photographed wearing the most beautiful creations in all the magazines. And perhaps Paul would fall in love with her. Pictured the headlines — 'Paul Melandes the wealthy chairman of Melandes Fashions marries Channel Islander'. Would he like children?

'Here we are, Miss.' The taxi driver's voice cut in on her dreams. He shook his head as she opened her bag. 'All paid for, Miss, goodnight.' For a few seconds Sorelle watched it leave. Everything was made so easy — at least to look easy by Paul. Nothing to worry about, even the taxi was paid for her and her car to be returned to her in the morning. He certainly had brought a new dimension to her life — had turned her world upside down.

She tumbled into bed, her body tired but her mind restless. Could still feel the impact on her mouth from his last savage kiss. Remembered what Ann had said about him being a collector. She could not have put the warning more plainly. And what happened to things that were collected? They were brought out occasionally, admired, then dusted and put away again. Or perhaps got pushed further and further into the background to make room for new objects.

Sorelle plumped her pillow under the sobering influence of her thoughts. Damn the man for interfering in her life. She had been tolerably happy before. Now her mind was criss-crossed with doubts. A decision had to be made by the time she met him in the morning. She turned on her back and pulled the bed covering to her, wishing that it was Paul to relieve the aching desire that he had aroused in her.

4

At about half-past eleven the next morning found them walking hand in hand along the cliff path which led from the town to Fermain Bay. He had expressed his wish again to see some more of the island on foot, and she having to be at the hotel for three o'clock had decided that Fermain would be ideal — not being too far away. They had parked the Mercedes near the beginning of the walk. At times the winding undulating path became narrow with the glinting blue sea far below on their left. Tall trees formed a background of different shades of green, reminding Sorelle of a theatre backdrop.

It was hot already and she was glad that she had dressed lightly in a short-sleeved simple open-necked blue dress with a white belt and sandals. A blue bandanna kept her hair in place. She had left her bag containing her work uniform in the car.

She glanced at him as he handed her down a steeper part, shiny hard roots above a scattering of last year's leaves on the well-worn path. He was beautiful, gorgeous, his white sports shirt and light grey trousers appearing to have been moulded to his athletic body. They had not spoken much, content to wander along in each other's company amidst the lovely surroundings. She thrilled with a sensuous delight when she knew that Paul was admiring her curves under the thin material of her dress.

They looked down on Fermain Bay — a sloping crescent of pebble and sand uncluttered by rocks, with its old tower and lovely wooded valley behind it. On such a day a paradise of yellow, blue and green. Then they had a coffee each, seated outside the small cafe, and Sorelle could not help noticing the glances her escort was receiving from scantily clad women. What if she were married to such a man, would not life be a succession of jealous daggers at her heart — a constant worry that arms other than hers would be enfolding him?

Afterwards they watched the ferry come in from St Peter Port, the passengers stepping on to the beach from the old, wheeled boarding platform. They waded the length of the bay in the shallows, his arm tightly around her, the uneven shore and the sea urging and pushing them against each other. She reminded herself that other women were waiting for him elsewhere no doubt. She must enjoy every second while it lasted. Enjoy the heavenly physical sensations this man conjured up in her. Love would be somewhere else.

Then to Sorelle's regret it was time to retrace their steps back to St Peter Port. Another hour and a half and would she ever see Paul again? If she refused his offer to work it was quite possible that she would not. After his European tour he would return home to America. She wondered what his home was like. Did he live alone? It was surprising to find that she knew very little about him.

They stopped to admire the view at a high point of the path, saw the white sails of a yacht in the summer haze. 'I've fallen for your island — it's beautiful.' She turned to him smiling her pleasure to find him staring at her, his eyes holding a haze of their own, 'And so are you,' he murmured throatily.

In a moment she was tightly held against him not knowing how it had happened, nor caring. Lost in his embrace under the sun. Suddenly he let her go, interrupted by people approaching. When they had passed he led her to a secluded place screened by gorse bushes from the path. They sat down on the soft tufty grass, the trees about providing welcome shade.

Sorelle sat primly, but eager for the touch of his lips again. The kiss on the path earlier had set a tide moving in her. She knew his eyes were probing her profile as he forced her gently against the soft earth. 'I shall never forget my time in Guernsey, Sorelle,' he breathed, 'something very special has happened to me here.' At the touch of his hand on her shoulder she reacted like a nervous filly, jerkily, tense and expectant, then his mouth imprisoned hers again.

His lips gentle and caressing at first grew progressively more dominating and passionate, and under the mounting influence of her emotions she pushed her breasts upward against him. Felt the male hardness of him through her thin clothes. Through half closed eyes she saw the trees appear to bend in over them, their tops beginning to revolve ever faster about the sky. Suddenly her lips were free. Surprised she saw that Paul had raised his head and was leaning over her, stared down at her for a few moments. Her senses tottered, her body aching for the contact with his again.

He glanced at his watch. 'I mustn't make you late for work, even though you're not going to be there much longer,' he uttered thickly. The word work brought her back from near heaven to earth, and with his help she rose unsteadily to her feet.

During the remainder of the way back to the car she tried to get some sort of order into her thoughts. He had made it obvious by his latter remark that he expected her to join his company, although he had not asked for her decision yet. Her mind cried out at the unfairness of it all — at his cruelty. Had he played upon her emotions in the hope that she would agree? A feeling of irritation and shame ran through her. Was she a toy that he could pick up and play with? Arouse her then carelessly put her aside. Did she mean so little to him? Was he so unaware of the emotions that he had stirred in her? Colour flooded her already hot face. She had been nearer to surrendering herself utterly than with any other man she had known. And in the daylight not five yards from a public path! He must think her easy prey. Too easy in fact to interest him further.

She was wrong. That enigmatic perplexing man dropped her outside the hotel, then, giving her no time to disagree, said he'd call for her at ten-thirty the following morning.

The day had not yet finished with its surprises however, because later in the afternoon Patti from the hotel boutique came to the reception desk. Eyed Sorelle in envious admiration. 'How d'you manage it? What have you got that I haven't?' Sorelle stared at her blankly. 'Don't be coy. I won't tell. Who is he? You know, that gorgeous hunk of man that came into my shop this morning.'

Sorelle struggled then gave up. 'I'm sorry Patti — I wasn't here this morning — I was off.'

'That dress you got from me, remember?'

Sorelle nodded, still perplexed. 'Well

he's paid the full amount for it so I'm returning the money you've paid already.'

'What was he like?' She knew even before the words were spoke

Patti sighed. 'American — classy. About seven feet, lean, dark. Didn't give his name. White shirt, grey slacks I think.' She gazed wonderingly at Sorelle. 'If that's what that dress got for you, I'm going to buy myself one.'

Sorelle stared at the money on the desk top. Paul had bought the dress for her. She remembered him admiring it, also herself saying that she had not yet paid fully for it.

Patti began to move away. 'If you see another like him tell me quick — don't let him get away.'

'I won't, and thanks,' smiled Sorelle. Stared after the other, happy and surprised that Paul had paid for it. It had been him, of that she was sure. But then a thought struck her bringing a niggling dissatisfaction and annoyance at herself. When she had informed Paul that it was not fully paid for, she had intended it just as an innocent remark.

She decided that when she saw him the next day she would thank him, but offer to repay him. He was rich, but that was not to say he had to give his money away. She smiled to herself, he hadn't mentioned anything to her about coming into the hotel that morning to her. Knowing that she was not on duty he had taken the opportunity to visit the boutique.

The following day Paul took her to lunch at the Belle Vue Hotel. They sat outside at a table on the lawn near an old well. Under a cloudless sky with the gentle breeze stirring the trees and tempering the midday sun. It was a perfect day and sitting opposite her a perfect man to go with it.

Paul lifted the bottle, let it hover over her glass. His eyes, a true hazel outdoors, challenged hers. 'Help me finish the wine, Sorelle.'

She refused with a giggle. 'If I have any more, I'll never return to work, but

I do thank you for the lunch and everything. I just wish that I could stay here all day.'

'Just ring your hotel and tell them you're coming with me — you won't be working for them any more,' Paul said easily, observing her.

Sorelle knew she must give him her decision soon. Her mind was already almost made up. She must not lose the company of the most stimulating man she had ever met. Then she remembered about the dress, leaned across the table towards him. 'Your secret is out. It was sweet and generous of you to buy the dress for me, but you shouldn't have.'

'Oh, why not?' He studied her over the rim of his glass.

'Well, it's not fair to you and — er . . . ' Sorelle struggled. 'You hardly know me.'

'Hardly know you.' Paul burst into a short deep laugh, moved towards her, grasped her hands in his large brown ones. 'I catch you twice when you fall, save you in the sea once, and you say I hardly know you. I may have to save you from something else yet.'

Sorelle couldn't help smiling. 'Well, all right then,' she gave in, 'but it was very kind of you.'

'You gained pleasure from wearing the dress didn't you?'

She nodded, remembering that it had made her feel wonderful.

'And I had the pleasure of seeing you in it,' he murmured softly. His lips were very close to hers across the table. She saw that people at other tables were casting curious and admiring looks at the handsome American.

For a while they sat there, she telling him of her family, where they were — what they did. Paul in turn told her about a new range of goods they were going to introduce into Europe. He did not she noticed reveal any more about himself that she did not already know.

Then he reached out, pulled her gently to her feet. 'How about a swim now in that inviting looking water before I take you back,' he suggested, nodding in the direction of the hotel swimming-pool. Sorelle was prepared, having her swimsuit on under her dress. Paul had told her to bring it, that they might go for a swim somewhere. She had thought it would be from one of the beaches. They crossed the lawn to fetch the bag holding the towels from the red Mercedes, open and gleaming in the sun on the hotel forecourt. She noticed the feminine eyes that were attracted to the figure of her companion.

There was nobody in the pool, just one man reclining on a sun bed at its edge. A small summer house stood at one side. She looked at Paul already beginning to strip off his shirt, tried to keep her eyes on his face and not on his tanned, taut, bare upper body.

'I thought only the residents could use the pool,' she said.

He gazed at her with a knowing tolerant humour from one of the loungers he had selected for them.

'When I phoned for a lunch reservation I made arrangements for us to have a dip if we wished.'

Sorelle undressed in the summer-house thinking about her companion. He was so self-assured, smooth and world wise. When she came out he was stood by the side of the pool, magnificent in very brief yellow trunks which left little to her imagination — being quite unable to conceal his masculine outline. He waited and watched as she came up to him. She felt as if she were a beauty parade contestant — one entrant and one judge. He missed nothing — she was sure of that, and by the look in his eyes she had won that particular contest. Her costume was a red one-piece, cut high and revealingly at the hips.

Paul plunged in arrow straight, then turned to watch her as she waded in down the steps, and allowed herself to slide into the cooling water. For some minutes they played like a pair of seals, nudging, touching, enjoying the freedom of the pool, she finding a delight in his excuse to caress her limbs as he showed her the finer points of the front crawl. Oh, why did she have to go back to work and leave this idyllic place?

She set off leisurely for the other end. Reaching it she remained immersed to her shoulders lightly grasping the edge of the pool. Almost hidden from the view of people sitting at the tables on the lawn. She heard the splash of Paul following. Suddenly felt his arms around her from behind. Locked like that for an ecstatic few moments, his palms in a caressing mould over her breasts. Turning in his arms she uttered a sigh which was silenced by his lips crushing hers. They clung thus, his hardening pressure sending her into a mounting rapture. Felt his heart hammering through her as he pressed so close that she thought no water could come between their bodies. She was becoming engulfed in a watery cocoon of desire.

A child's voice calling to someone broke the spell. Sorelle opened her eyes. The man on the sun bed was still dozing, and she could hear the muted talk from the diners at the tables.

'When is your day off?' Paul spoke with an effort, husky-voiced, recovering from the bout of desire that had gripped him.

Sorelle's mind struggled into the every day again. 'Er — Thursday, I think, yes Thursday.'

He was breathing quickly and there was a peculiar light in his eyes. 'Dinner on the *Privateer* then — Thursday — say eight-thirty. Taxi will call for you,' he said in staccato fashion.

She nodded. Paul Melandes had a habit of making up your mind for you. And anyway she felt in no mood to disagree.

Back in the car again Sorelle sank back into her seat stretching luxuriously, noticing the glances thrown their way. One thing was certain, the man by her side at the wheel certainly did a lot for her confidence. He had now put on dark sun-glasses. Perhaps they thought that he was a film star and that she was too. She smiled wistfully to herself as they turned out of the hotel gates. Just a receptionist who must keep her feet firmly on the ground. Her heart beat faster. At dinner on the yacht he would most certainly want to know her decision. She had already made it.

After work that night she was tired but not too tired to go over again that wonderful few hours she had shared earlier in the day with Paul. Magical moments that she would remember for ever. The feel of his arms around her in the hotel pool, and her very real awareness of his powerful virility. Their kiss in the water. Was it possible that he was beginning to feel as she had felt for some time now, that it was more than just an intense physical attraction? She was falling in love — no — had fallen from the first time she had seen him, she realised. Perhaps it was foolish, naïve and school-girlish. Yet it had happened so swiftly. But was she making a prison for her own heart by thinking that he may also look on her as more than just another plaything?

She remembered the woman Ann's remarks about him — a collector, she had called him. The word had a cynical, lifeless, loveless sound. Was it possible he was just a pitiless, shallow seeker of sensual thrills? Only in love with his work. Yet she tried to convince herself that the looks, glances, touches, his slow enchanting smile, the pressure of his body and lips on hers must mean that he regarded her as more than just an object of rampant desire.

On at least one occasion they had been private enough for him to make physical love to her, and if he had she could not have resisted him. He must have guessed. Now on Thursday she was to dine on his yacht with him. She was going to enter the tiger's cage defenceless — her heart captured already. No doubt they would discuss the position he had offered her and she would accept it. But that was an excuse for her, she knew, to be near him. In reality she was hoping that he would tell her that he loved her and wanted her to stay with him and share his life. But anything less than that and she ran the risk of acquiring a scar on her heart which may never heal.

The next day Sorelle gave a week's notice in at work. The manager was very surprised, sorry that she was going and so soon. He asked whether she had another job to go to. Modelling, she told him, and that she might be leaving the island. Rather a precarious profession, he thought. Was it one of the big fashion houses? Melandes. Wasn't he on the island at present?

The manager looked at the exciting shining eyes of the young woman opposite him. He was old enough to know the signs. Guessed that it wasn't the job but a man that had brought that light into her eyes. He shrugged inwardly and told her that if it didn't work out she must contact him.

The deed was done. She realised that she would miss the island. Having returned and got to know her birthplace better, she was now going to leave. But the pervading and drawing force of Paul Melandes was exercising a more powerful influence over her — over her heart.

On the morning of her day off she went into town. It was too nice to stay in, and yet she did not feel like visiting a beach. Her mind was too concentrated on where she was going to be that coming evening. She sat sipping a coffee inside one of the esplanade cafés, and able to see the harbour and the world going by through the open grill work. If she stretched in her seat she could just see the *Privateer* at its moorings.

People continued to pass the café. Others leaning over the harbour rail gazing at the boats. Perhaps admiring Paul Melandes' yacht. They and the people at the other tables nearby could not know that she would be the guest on board that very yacht later that day. Her mouth began to dry and her pulse quickened. What would she be like at nine o'clock?

Afterwards she sat in Candie Gardens above the town with its views across the harbour to Herm and the other islands. Watched the almost imperceptible progress of the yachts and the white streaks of motor boat wakes in the blue expanse. The occasional couple passed her, arms around each other. And she thrilled at the prospect of Paul's arms around her again.

Restlessly she made her way down on to the Glategny Esplanade and then in the direction of St Sampsons, skirting Bellegreve Bay. The walk was quiet after the bustle and throng of the town, and occasionally she stopped and leaned on the sea wall and gazed over the water at the few isolated boats gently dipping at their moorings. But Sorelle did not see them, she was too busy asking herself the same question over and over. Had she been foolish in giving her notice so quickly — impulsively? She smiled wryly, acknowledging that the job he had offered was exciting, but that the real reason for her joining his company would be to be near him.

As she turned to retrace her steps another question always in her mind demanded an answer. Could a man like Paul Melandes possibly fall in love with her? Did such miracles happen? Or even now were Ann, Maurice and Scott making bets as to whether she would become the umpteenth conquest of the boss of Melandes Fashions?

5

At approximately nine-thirty that evening the taxi dropped her at the end of the jetty. The *Privateer's* boat was waiting for her at the bottom of the steps. The man in charge of it was the same one who had taken her across the night of the cocktail party. He welcomed her politely in a foreign accent and she felt that he was pleased to see her.

She was dressed almost exactly as she had been on her last visit in her brown mini dress and golden sandals. A forehead band with a small cluster of *diamantés* in the front kept her fair hair in place. A white knitted shoulder cape, its ends tied loosely at her throat, made a pretty contrast. Perhaps she would have worn something different for this her second visit, but Paul had insisted that she wear the same dress. He had admired it and had paid her more than one compliment during that other evening.

Paul was waiting for her at the bottom of the yacht's ladder. Welcomed her, his eyes as dark as the surrounding water and his hand quickly round hers, as he led her aboard. How quiet it seemed in comparison with the night of the cocktail party. There was no-one else in sight, and Sorelle wondered if apart from the man who had brought her across they were alone on the yacht.

Paul took her into the saloon. Romantic piano music came from somewhere. In a corner a table for two had been set. He then relieved her of her cape, gently untying its ends from behind her, his warm breath against the nape of her neck. 'A sherry?' His lips were close to her ear.

She nodded. Only a few minutes in his presence and she was already quivering with an anticipatory pleasure. He handed her the glass, his eyes missing nothing in their following, approving, appraisal of her. He raised his. 'To our association — may it flourish.' His eyes held hers above the rim. Yes, she'd drink to that, an association in which he fell in love with her — strictly non-business.

She wondered if he had any idea as to the real reason she was willing to join it. In a way she wished that she had had the strength to refuse his offer. But her heart was in a tangle whenever she was with him. He looked wonderful, masculine in a dark blue blazer, an open-neck white shirt and thigh-hugging white jeans.

They sat on a soft leather settee beneath a picture of what she guessed was the *Privateer* 'I gave my notice in yesterday,' she informed him.

'I knew you would. I'm glad, very glad. Welcome to the company, Sorelle.' Had she seen a flash of triumphant satisfaction? 'When d'you leave?'

'In a week, I gave them a week's notice.'

He must have heard some tiny doubt, anxiety in her. Took hold of her hands

'You're not having second thoughts already are you?' His gaze held some amusement.

She shook her head, her eyes having difficulty in leaving his. 'No, oh no, I'm thrilled — can't believe it.'

He nodded. 'Good. I like to run a happy ship. A business is like a ship, Sorelle. It won't run efficiently if the workers are not happy, or the management come to that,' he added drily.

Mention of the ship reminded her of the photograph above them. She stood up to have a closer look at it. 'This is the *Privateer* isn't it?'

'Yes, it was taken off the Portuguese coast on the way here, soon after I bought it.' She heard the ice tinkle in his drink. 'You should know the *Privateer* quite well now,' he said with a trace of mockery.

She knew what he meant. Implying it had been her intention all along to get on board from the first day. She wanted to be sarcastic in return. Instead she ignored his remark and turned to him, about to elicit some further information from him about his yacht. Caught the fleeting last of his expression as he observed her. Anything she was going to say remained unspoken. Her eyes must have told her wrongly. Surely she was mistaken. Cynical amusement had been reflected in his features, but in the narrow heavy-lidded gaze there had been a contempt. But his expression now was smilingly attentive, and interested in what she had been about to say.

Sorelle turned back to the picture quickly to hide the shock she had felt. 'W — whereabouts are we now on the boat?' she asked, her fingers hovering over the picture. Had that expression really been there? Or had she imagined it — a trick of the yacht's lights perhaps?

He picked up her cape and draped it around her shoulders, his fingertips lingering for a moment on the front of her dress just above her breasts. 'C'mon, I'll give you a short guided tour.' His hands were warm on her waist as he led her between the glass doors on to the after deck, then up a short flight of steps to a platform high above the water. 'This is the upper steering position for when the weather is fine,' he explained. 'Go on — take hold of the wheel.'

Sorelle took hold of it, looked down and along the enormous seeming length of the yacht. 'Some day I'll let you steer it.' Paul's voice came from behind her as he gently gripped her shoulders. She could feel the hard pressure of his knees against the backs of her thighs, his cheek against her hair. It was wonderful up there with him — high flying like her heart. She could see the lights of the other boats, the activity on the esplanade, and overhead the stars trying to match the reflections of the *Privateer's* lights in the water. The music came up clearly from the saloon below.

Paul turned her in his arms and brought her closer to him. Then they danced slowly, and the esplanade, the traffic, the harbour itself vanished for Sorelle. The world consisted of just she and this man. Nothing else mattered. Her head against the hard pad of his powerful chest.

'You and the *Privateer* have a lot in common,' he murmured, his lips caressing her ear.

'Oh.' It was all she could manage.

'Yes, you're both beautiful and graceful.'

She sighed against him at the compliment. Supposed it was a worthy one — he was proud of his boat. Would his feeling for her ever extend to something more than pride? His mouth found hers and her senses spun.

She would have remained there locked in his arms forever if he hadn't withdrawn his lips slowly and then began to lead her towards the steps to the after deck. 'The air up here gives me an appetite,' he uttered huskily. 'I'm sure it does you too.' It did, but the feelings she had had nothing to do with food.

Over dinner her senses began to settle down, and her mind began to work logically again, though a smile or a touch of his hand set off an excited disordered glow within her again. He was attentive, courteous, giving every appearance of being totally interested in what she had to say. It was difficult to believe that she had actually seen that look of contempt in his eyes earlier. In fact she told herself she could not have done. Sorelle also found it hard to believe that she was there at all, dining alone with Paul Melandes, the handsome boss of Melandes Fashion.

The man who served the dinner she noticed was the same one who had brought her across to the yacht. Middle-aged and foreign with kindly brown eyes. Over the sweet — pears in chilled white wine — she mentioned it to Paul.

'That's Carlos — he acts as my general help — a sea butler if you like, looks after me on board,' he explained. 'He came with the yacht almost. He's Portuguese, and he was out of work when I met him, just rotting away, so I took him on. The man's changed beyond recognition — he's happy and he's good at his work.' Sorelle's companion spread his hands palms upwards. 'We're both happy.' Once more she realised that under the ruthless business exterior he had a soft spot.

Then after ordering Carlos to bring the champagne to his cabin, he grasped Sorelle's hand and led her down a few steps into a narrow wood-panelled passage with thick carpet underfoot, their path lit by dark red lamps at intervals casting a cosy glow.

His broad-shouldered tall figure seemed to fill the passage ahead of her. He stopped and pushed open a door directly ahead. Stood aside and ushered her in with a flourish of his hands. 'Welcome to the captain's cabin — Captain Melandes at your service.' His eyes held a roguish gleam.

She glanced around her. A small squarish room, wood panelled as in other parts of the yacht she had seen. Softly lit with electricity from old-fashioned looking lanterns. It was sparsely furnished with a dark red curved couch, a desk and a small table, and a couple of upright chairs. A thick luxuriant red carpet cushioned Sorelle's feet. Gold-coloured curtains hung over windows at one side. She glimpsed the night outside between them. A masculine room — austere but having a warming effect.

Paul stood watching her. 'I know what you're going to tell me, it needs a woman's touch. Am I right?'

She nodded and smiled at the correctness of his guess. Would have liked to have been the woman to do it for him. The cabin did need a feminine touch — flowers and more colour. 'But it isn't a woman who lives in it, is it?' she answered thinking that anyone less womanly it would be hard to find.

Carlos appeared with a tray on which was a bottle of champagne and glasses. He placed them on the table then looked at his employer. 'You want something else, Mr Melandes?' he asked in his heavily accented tones.

'No, I think that's all Carlos thank you.' Carlos turned to leave. 'Wait Carlos,' said Paul after him, 'perhaps Miss Dalby would like a coffee later.' He regarded her with a lurking teasing humour.

Preferably black if she was going to drink some of that champagne first. But then she looked at the older man. Perhaps he'd had a long day. 'No, it's all right, Paul, there's no need for him to make it specially for me.'

'I'm sure he'll take great pleasure in making it just for you, won't you Carlos?'

The older man nodded and smiled — a tired smile. 'Yes, Mr Melandes.'

'I'll ring, Carlos, when we're ready.' Carlos closed the door behind him, but not before he had given a quick backward glance of approval at Sorelle. The latter moved the heavy curtains apart a few more inches, glanced out

126

into the darkness. Could see the great bulk of the floodlit Castle Cornet.

Paul took off his blazer and threw it over the settee and then picked up the bottle of champagne with a flourish. He gazed at her challengingly. 'Now let's drink to our success.' The subdued lighting and his white shirt accentuated his dark handsomeness. She thought he could have been a pirate about to drink a toast to another captured prize. It flashed through her mind that that was what she herself could be — a prize for a man who specialised in capturing hearts. And yet she felt incapable just then of resisting, or indeed of wishing to. Paul Melandes held a fascination for her which was overpowering and at that moment she wanted to be possessed. She was in a world quite different to the one she had been used to, and was determined to enjoy the sensations and thrills that went with it.

She felt the slight movement of the *Privateer* beneath her. Wondered if the yacht liked her. Knew it was a foolish thought, but could it resent another woman coming aboard? Could a boat be jealous? The yacht's movement had caused a door opposite to swing open. Sorelle glimpsed a bed — a large one — too large for one man. She imagined Margot and others in it with Paul. The voice inside her — a very tiny one, trying to make itself heard. Don't be a fool it said. Thank him for the evening, call it off now whilst you've still time. Don't let it go any further. Say goodbye to this man.

Paul began to open the bottle, his short sleeves revealing the play of rippling muscular arms. The cork popped, hit the cabin ceiling with a crack then landed by the door. The liquid sparkled and bubbled as it rose in her glass, expressive of the happiness rising in her at that moment.

'To our success, Paul.' It sounded good to say 'our success'. Brought him closer to her. A moment later he had translated that into fact, seating her gently on the couch and he settling himself half turned against her. A tremor of sensuous delight coursed through her at his nearness. He must notice she thought how unsteady the champagne had become in her glass.

She gazed out of her vivid blue eyes into the ones that were now trained on her, and making it extremely difficult for her to concentrate. Something she wanted to ask him. 'Paul, where shall I live when I come to work for you?' Wondered if he would think she had hoped to live on the yacht.

He shrugged slightly. 'Where you are living now — for part of the time anyway. There's accommodation in the cities where we shall be showing our merchandise. I'll let you know.'

Sorelle was surprised and somewhat disappointed. She had imagined that she would have had to go away with him — travel with him, would have wished for that, but his tone had been off-hand and dismissive of the matter.

'Has that surprised you, Sorelle?' His compelling eyes seemed to chase her innermost thoughts and capture them. She was glad of the low lights to hide her discomfiture. Before she could answer he added, 'I would have thought that you would not want to leave such a gorgeous island.'

She would have left almost anything for him. 'I suppose that's true, it would be a wrench, but if the job means I've got to leave then I would,' she said as matter of factly as she could manage. Strangely, she felt a small relief that she would not have to leave the island immediately. In her heart of hearts what she really wanted was for him to marry her and buy a house on the island and live happily ever after. But that was a dream, and no doubt would remain so. She sighed inwardly then became aware that he was topping up her glass with more champagne.

She would have to be careful. A mocking voice inside her head told her it was too late to worry about that. A second one joined in. Where was Margot? What had he done with her?

Or did they have some arrangement so that when he did not have a new woman in tow she resumed her role of his mistress again?

Sorelle heard herself saying 'I suppose I'm not the only girl you've entertained aboard,' remembering too late that he had told her that he had bought the yacht in Portugal not so very long ago.

He eyed her over his glass. 'Well,' he drawled drily, 'you could say there's safety in numbers.' He put his drink down on the table and leaned towards her, his fingers touching the lobe of her ear and then trailing gossamer-like down the side of her throat. A simple movement, but it set up in Sorelle a craving for him to continue. His eyes seemed to sap her mind of everything but that. 'You're unique. I invited you here tonight — no-one else. If I'd wanted someone else they would have been here, not you.' His fingers remained on her throat caressing its length. 'I couldn't do without you now,

Sorelle. You're right for me — I know it,' he whispered.

His words transported her into a world where dreams come true. Only she and this man mattered in the universe at that precise moment. His lips teased hers gently, stoking the animal fire rising inside her. Through hazy half-opened eyes she saw him draw back to gaze on her, but resenting even that momentary time his mouth was away from hers. She guessed he was seeing her almost naked as he had done that day at Moulin Huet from his boat. Melting away her dress with his eyes and seeing her in intimate detail.

His mouth descended on hers briefly but harder this time, then lingered on her arched throat. Her lips searched for his unable to bear the exquisite cruelty of their parting again. Her arms as if by a will of their own crept around Paul's head, her fingertips ploughing a caress through his hair. He leaned over her, his hand in the small of her back moulding her willing body against him.

She made a sound in her throat — a plea for his mouth to cover hers again. Never had she felt such a craving ever before in a man's arms. The urgent pain of unfulfilment. When their lips met again she worked hers against his as if it was the last kiss she would have on earth. The boat was floating not on water, but in time and space.

He found the zip of her dress and drew it down slowly over her shoulders. The tension in her was unbearable as she strained under the intimate caress of her breasts, their nipples like the tips of volcanoes ready to burst with the spiralling fire of desire beneath, and teased between his fingers gentle as an alighting butterfly. Then Paul's hand was warm and large upon the front of her waist. Anticipation joined the intensity of her emotion and her body moved eagerly.

How long their kiss lasted she did not know or care. She was lost to everything but the man crushing her in his embrace. It was as if his lips were

133

sucking every last vestige of resistance from her, poised and waiting for his more intimate caresses — brought to a fever pitch. His mouth left hers and she sighed petulantly like a child when its toy is taken away, dimly aware of him lifting her easily from the couch and walking with her limp in his arms, her head against his chest. He laid her on the bed.

Sorelle waited impatiently for his touch again and the full weight of him to crush her to the bed. The desire he had stirred and stoked in her needed satisfying totally. After a few seconds and with an effort she half opened her eyes.

Paul was leaning over her staring down at her, hands either side of her. Oh Paul, love me, her mind screamed. Then her vision cleared and she saw his expression more clearly and even in the half light there was no mistaking it. Beneath the haze of his desire it held that which she had seen earlier — contempt — but now a grudging admiration was also present. Anxiety damped the flames of passion still hot within her. 'What's the matter?' she whispered staring up at him. It seemed a long time since she had used her voice.

He smiled slowly, a strangely sad disappointed smile. 'Nothing's the matter — for you.'

Sorelle tried to cleave her way back to full alertness, her desire ebbing away swiftly. What was he talking about? Tried to comprehend.

Paul continued to gaze down on her reflectively. 'Funny, I couldn't believe it when I first saw you, you're so much alike in looks.' His tone was tender with a note of surprise running through it. 'I didn't think it possible. I couldn't believe my luck. Like her in looks but different inside.' His lips twisted wryly, eyes questioning hers. 'But you never can tell can you!'

Anxiety had turned into a gnawing sickness of heart. 'What d'you mean?' she asked tremulously. Her dream was beginning to fade.

'It doesn't matter Sorelle, my honey.' His lips curved though they held no real warmth. 'But I'll tell you this, you made me fall for you — I really fell for you, make no mistake about that. I thought you were the real genuine article.' Bitterness had begun to edge his words.

What was happening to her? What had happened to them?

'I thought I could spot the gold-diggers a mile off, always have.' He touched her cheek with his fingers. She flinched under his touch and words. Aghast and too confused to speak for the moment. Her fingers felt for reassurance, but found only evidence of the bed she lay on.

He continued to speak as if to a child — a child whose being was chilling with every passing moment. 'But don't worry, Sorelle. You can work for me and have a good time. I'll keep you on — you deserve that much I guess. But don't expect anything else — like marriage.' His hand rested on the swell of her stomach in a proprietary way, eyes emptied of everything but lust. His mouth descended to pin hers.

Sorelle twisted her head, shocked and cold inside herself where moments before she had been warm and giving with love for him. Squirmed quickly from beneath him to stand facing him on the other side of the bed, anger and misery etched on her face. 'How dare you talk to me like that? I'm not a gold-digger,' she flung at him, her voice choked with emotion, her eyes blazing in a sudden blue fury. All she had dreaded was happening to her.

Surprise gave way to interested amusement on Paul's face. 'The lady has spirit, this is going to be fun.'

'Fun, yes that's all you think it is don't you, just fun to you. To be spoken about as if I were a horse or a boat or . . . ' She stopped, gazed at him in a terrible despair. That god of a man she had built her life around during the last few weeks — weaved dreams for them both. Now he had destroyed everything and she was shattered by the realisation of what he was really like and of what he thought of her. Angry at herself for believing otherwise after she had been warned about getting too close to the candle of love when it was held out to her by a man like Paul Melandes.

His expression had hardened with a touch of puzzled surprise. 'This is what you wanted isn't it?' Glance and gesture encompassed the cabin and bed. 'You've made it — a lot don't, I'm choosy. What's all the histrionics for? What did you expect? Marriage tomorrow and a half share in the business also?' He made to come round to her side of the bed.

'Don't touch me,' she shot at him, stepping back.

'D'you mean to tell me that all this time you'd thought I'd fallen in love with you?' His eyes glinted with a cruel incredulity.

'I don't care what I meant to tell you,' she cried, the flood gates of her distress and anger opening fully. 'It doesn't matter any more. You just think that you can do anything you want. Hurt people's feelings, ride roughshod over them. You think you can buy them — give them a good time and they're yours. Well, not all women are like that — me for one. Has it ever crossed your egotistical swollen head that someone can like a person and be content with what that person is — not for what they can get out of them.'

She saw his eyes move downwards, became aware of her near naked upper body, her breasts quivering with the strength of her voiced emotions. Pulling her dress up around her shoulders savagely she made for the door.

Paul blocked her way. Caught her by the arm roughly, his powerful grasp stopping her easily. 'Wait,' he ordered, 'you can't go far anyway. Have you forgotten where you are?'

'No I haven't and I want to get off it as quickly as possible. No way do I want to spend another minute on this yacht.' She struggled against him. 'Let me go. I never want to see you again. As far as I'm concerned you're empty, conceited and just an animal.' She saw his nostrils flare, the anger flicker in his piercing gaze.

'Don't you want to model for me?'

'Damn your modelling, and you with it. I've done all the modelling I'm going to do for you, tonight.'

'Don't tell me that you weren't just a little bit attracted by the aura of the rich.' His tone was scathing.

Sorelle was hurt and it showed. She tried to calm herself. 'Maybe, but the man mattered an awful lot more. You'd have been the same without your yacht and your money to me.' Remembered her grandmother's dictum of trying to preserve some dignity whatever the circumstances. It was difficult in her present one.

He gripped her hard, making her wince, anger smouldering in his eyes as they bored into hers. 'Look, the only reason you're hysterical is because I told you the truth and you don't like it — isn't that so?'

She tried again to free herself, twisted in his grasp. 'No it isn't. I'm hurt yes, but not for that reason, it will be beyond you to appreciate why. Now let me go.' To her surprise he did and she stood panting, her breasts heaving with her emotion.

A smile appeared but it contained little tenderness, only a lurking frustrated desire in his regard of her. 'You won't be the first good-time girl, and you're as beautiful as they come.' His voice became lower, softly persuasive. 'Don't let's spoil it, Sorelle. What's so wrong with having yourself fun?' He twisted the knife. 'Love is for the movies.'

'What you really mean is I shouldn't spoil your fun. You don't care a button for my feelings, all you want is somebody — I mean somebody to fill the place next to you on that bed. Any woman will do provided she's got a passable face — it's the body that

141

counts isn't it? Well this is one good-time girl that's throwing you over.' She wanted to hurt him like he'd hurt her. 'D'you know what your problem is, Paul? You're blaming the whole of my sex because one woman let you down. Do you have to go on taking revenge on every woman you fancy? When will it stop?' Sorelle saw his rising terrible anger in the face opposite.

With a choking sob she ran from the bedroom into the cabin. There she trod on something. Saw that it was the cork from the bottle of champagne which Paul had opened earlier — it had signified the reaching of another level of happiness for her in their relationship. The sight of the cork only made her feel more wretched. There had been a different look on Paul's face then from the one she had just seen.

She found herself in the passage outside. Stumbled up the steps into the state room, the table where they had dined now cleared and lonely. Glimpsed Carlos out of the corner of

142

her eyes as she hurried through the saloon and on to the after deck. She could see nobody in attendance on the yacht's boat bobbing gently below. How was she going to get ashore? Remembered that it was Carlos who had brought her. She shivered, not having stopped to pick up her cape. Hesitating, she half turned back then saw Carlos — he must have followed her, anxiety and astonishment showing on his dark features. 'Carlos, please take ... ' Sorelle stopped. Paul had appeared behind him carrying her cape. She felt foolish, immature.

He handed it to Carlos, addressed him. 'Miss Dalby wishes to leave, Carlos. See that she gets a cab.' His voice was icy and level, his features etched in a white iron under the deck lights.

With a desperate sadness Sorelle glanced at him, then hardly able to hold back tears followed Carlos down the ladder and into the boat. And the *Privateer*'s lights reflected in the water which had lit her coming so happily were now mocking gleeful eyes dancing at her misery.

Carlos kindly waited until the taxi arrived. She thought he understood. The town church clock struck its time, the notes a sombre final musical curtain to her dream of love. Back in her flat she hardly had the will to prepare for bed, but just crumpled on to it, and gave vent to her frustrated and pent-up feelings.

One thing seemed certain — their time together over the last few days when she imagined that he might have a growing love for her, had meant just one thing to him — the prelude and preparation for getting her into his bed. The affair had meant nothing more to him, something he had been doing a long time, and would no doubt continue doing with any woman who caught his eye.

Sorelle's face grew hot at the thought of how abandoned she had been with him. His influence over her had been so powerful, so magnetic that she had not had a will of her own. Had known the danger and chance of heartbreak, but had taken the gamble and lost. She had been conceited enough to suppose that she could change him, to be the one that he would love completely and solely. But she had been easy for him — no wonder he had thought she was just a good-time girl. Sorelle bridled again in a return of anger. It had been uncalled-for and cruel. He had been so sure of her.

She lay down weary and drained. How could he have kissed her like he had — his soul in his lips and yet not meant it? A comet of love had flashed from the heavens, borne her along on its starway, then had returned her to earth much too quickly.

6

It was an anxious and heavy-hearted Sorelle that walked into the Longchamps Hotel the next day. To her relief the manager accepted her withdrawal of her week's notice. It was an empty relief anyway, a return to second best after discovering something that had set her life alight. She settled down again to the routine of work with a dull far-away look in her eyes. The others guessed and comforted her. 'Never mind Sorelle, there'll be another one.' There would but she would never feel about another as she had in her relationship with Paul Melandes.

When she returned home that evening a large bouquet of red and white roses awaited her on the doorstep. She knew who they were from. Another bouquet, even larger, of red roses arrived at the hotel the following midday. Just as she had with the first she ignored the yacht's telephone number on the card attached.

Red roses, the emblem of love between man and woman. Sent by a man who had as good as told her that love did not enter into his relationship with a woman. But she, Sorelle, was looking for a deeper more lasting kind of relationship. Paul Melandes was not prepared to, or could not enter into the kind of loving bond that Sorelle as a woman wanted. Sadly she let the other girls split the bouquet between them. They thought she was crazy — perhaps she was.

It was with something of a shock two days later that she found that the *Privateer* had vanished from its place in the harbour. Life seemed empty, lonely. It was the end of a beautiful dream. On her day off — a glorious blue-skied hot day, she took her car and drove to Vazon Bay. She could not bear to go to Moulin Huet or Fermain Bay — they would remind her too much of the man who had just gone from her life.

Sadly she sat on the steps by the sea wall and stared at the white lines of gentle rollers washing the huge golden crescent of sand. She began to wonder if she had not been too hasty and easily offended. Had Paul Melandes been right when he had said that she was hurt because he had told her the truth? No, even that first day on the esplanade, he had in those few moments already made an impact on her heart, and she had no idea then that he was very wealthy.

And what about his feelings? Had she not said things that had obviously been offensive to him. What he had done before in his life was no concern of hers. Sorelle cringed inside herself at the memory. Sighed heavily with a regretful longing. What a poor thing he must have thought her after all the sophisticated women he must have known. She had not even replied to his gifts of flowers. Could at least have hidden the scars on her heart and thanked him and wished him well. It was too late now. She got up to go back to the car, her eyes moist.

The next month Sorelle was kept busy, it being the height of the holiday season. During the day her mind was occupied with hotel business, and to some extent she forgot there had ever been a man called Paul Melandes. But at night alone it was a different matter — remembering his face, his piercing, though usually friendly eyes, the fit of his clothes, the feel of his body when they had been pressed close together. But, she would have to face the fact that the affair was finished. She couldn't go about carrying a torch for a man she would never see again.

One afternoon in early September Sorelle glanced casually at the bundle of copies of the *Guernsey Press* — the local newspaper. The hotel always purchased some for visitors who may be interested to read about the island's affairs. The top copy had sprung apart revealing the upper section of the leader page. Suddenly her eyes were arrested in their idle traversing of the print. The words seemed to grow into a three-dimensional form standing out in blocks from the paper.

'Millionaire in deal to buy island. Mr Paul Melandes, the American millionaire head of Melandes Fashions, has been having talks with the Guernsey States about the purchase of Ormer Island. Mr Melandes visited the Channel Islands — in particular Guernsey — earlier in the summer and is said to have been captivated by its charm and beauty. Ormer Island' the report went on 'has been inhabited before, but when the last owner died the house on it fell into disrepair. No price has yet been mentioned but estimates place the total value at somewhere near half a million pounds.'

Sorelle picked up the edge of the paper, it shaking in time to her suddenly thudding heart. She sat down, her legs trembling with shock at the news. For a few moments her mind became a kaleidoscope of words, sights and sounds that she had experienced when in the company of Paul Melandes. Joy that he was going to be living in the vicinity raced through her. Her true feelings were revealed to herself in those few moments. Given the chance she would now do anything to attain the relationship that she had had with him before their quarrel. He was returning — the man she thought was gone for ever.

But what of him? Common sense poured a chilling douche of cold reasoning upon her, all but extinguishing the fire of excitement that had flared so easily within her. What was she to him now? Nothing. She had cut herself off from him. In any case she was certain she had never meant a great deal to him, apart from being an object of sexual interest. Not even that now. Wild ideas of hope came and went.

And yet the excitement that had arisen in her on first seeing the newspaper report did not fade entirely.

Her imagination pictured him as she had seen him last, but with one alteration. His angry set face had gone, replaced with the warm, attentive, slow-smiling hazel-eyed one. As it had been when they had dined that day and swum at the Belle Vue Hotel. Sorelle smiled. Just like him to go and buy an island — a whole island, not just the house on it. His fault was in thinking that he could buy every heart also.

The report did not go unnoticed by the others at work. 'He's come back to fetch you, Sorelle. You never know, wedding bells could be ringing yet.' Oh, if only that were true! For him to come and say he loved her.

That evening she took her car into town unable to resist the urge to find out where the *Privateer* was berthed, telling herself that all she wanted to do was to see it — that was all. Just curiosity. Going down the Grange it suddenly struck her that he may not have brought the yacht. In fact he may not be in Guernsey at all. He could be arranging his business from the Continent or London, or anywhere for that matter. She wondered when he had gone to Ormer Island. He would not have bought it without going over it surely.

There was no sign of the *Privateer* in the inner or outer town harbour. It crossed her mind that it could be at St Sampsons. She carried on past the bus terminus with its old-fashioned green coaches, then parked her car near the wall of Havelet Bay. The air was warm as she got out and stretched against the wall to look over.

The *Privateer* rode quietly at anchor, the name plain on the stern, half turned towards her. White with a shading of pink from the lowering sun. Behind it the castle walls loomed solid and darker in the near distance. A few small open craft bobbed about in attendance at a respectful distance. Sorelle felt a powerful thrill surge through her. Paul was here, in the island! Was he on board? She strained her eyes but could not see anyone on deck. She turned away and got back into the car, glad of it to hide the sadness which had suddenly come over her and more heartache.

Sunday was her change-over day and she walked in just before three o'clock. Stella looked at her curiously. 'You've had a phone call this morning.'

'Oh.' Her mind went to her mother and John. Occasionally they phoned to see how she was.

'Yes, a woman. Wanted to know if you were on duty today. I told her that you were later. Did I do right?'

'Didn't she give her name?' Couldn't be her family, they would have said immediately who they were.

'No,' said Stella, 'not the first time, anyway.'

'How d'you mean?' Sorelle showed her puzzlement, couldn't quite understand the gleam of mischief in the other's regard.

'She rang again not long afterwards — I'm sure it was the same woman. Booked a table for tonight.'

'Well, what made you think it was the same person?'

'She had an American accent — not a very pronounced one, just a nice one I thought.'

'American!' Sorelle's heart jumped into her mouth at the information.

'Yes.' Stella's look had become knowing.

'What name was it booked under?' She had guessed already.

'Melandes — Paul Melandes. Isn't he the one that's thinking of buying Ormer Island? I'm sure I read it somewhere.'

Sorelle nodded dumbly, an array of emotions passing through her.

'Wasn't he the one who sent you the flowers?' Stella whistled in wonder. 'It's not every day you find a man who buys an island.' She patted Sorelle on the shoulder as she prepared to go, gave her a bright encouraging smile. 'I shouldn't be surprised if he hasn't booked that table for the two of you. You never know, see you tomorrow.'

Sorelle looked after her retreating form unseeingly, her mind in a turmoil.

Drawn to and excited by him on the one hand, yet embarrassed and awkward about seeing him again. How could she avoid seeing him — there was no way she could hide, nor could she be quite sure of his time of arrival, though Stella had mentioned the table was booked for nine o'clock. In that case she, Sorelle, would be extremely busy between quarter to nine and half past, head bent over anything she could find, or hopefully engaged on the telephone repeatedly during that time.

A table for two — no doubt another woman she reflected somewhat bitterly. Someone else had soon taken her place. Why oh why had he elected to come to dinner at that hotel? There were dozens of hotels and restaurants he could have chosen from. Was he doing it deliberately to flaunt another conquest in front of her — humiliate her? If he was, then it was another objectionable facet of his character that was being revealed.

Nevertheless, as the hour approached so her heart began to hammer a quicker beat. She could already feel a dynamic and magnetic force at work on her. Tried to fight it, arranging brochures, travel documents, checking arrivals and departure lists, keeping her face well hidden. How bright the reception lights were — she'd never noticed them before. She felt like a figure in a presentation case — on view. Her eyes stole to the clock — nine-fifteen. If only someone could engage her in conversation for a while. She bent lower.

'Good evening, Sorelle.' The deep sensual voice invaded her being, drawing her gaze upward as if she had no will of her own. For a fleeting moment his glance rode over her. She was aware of his deep tan against the fawn of his suit. His female companion was a dark-haired striking-looking handsome woman in crimson, about the same age or perhaps a little older than he was with a vibrant expressive face. Then they were gone, his short wave like the signal for the end of her once beautiful dream.

Sorelle slumped weakly, elbows on her desk. Perhaps she would be gone before they left the restaurant. Oh, how could he be so callous and cruel, torturing her by bringing another woman, parading his new love in front of her. Fortunately for a while she was kept busy, giving her subconcious time to analyse the brief encounter more closely, so that when she had time to reflect again a rather perplexing fact emerged. The woman with Paul had not appeared surprised or annoyed at his greeting to a younger woman in such obviously familiar tones. The more Sorelle recalled the expression on his companion's face the more puzzled she became. The woman in the short time they were passing reception had looked at her in an appraising way. No jealousy, no hard hands-off tigerish look that Margot had given. No, the look had definitely been softer — more searching than antagonistic.

But the fact remained that Paul had sought the company of another woman in preference to that of hers. Sorelle sighed — she couldn't really blame him — she herself had broken the affair up on the yacht. She did not see Paul or his companion again that evening and was glad to get away to the privacy of her flat where she could writhe inwardly with the pain from the re-opened wound in her heart.

The following day a note was awaiting her when she arrived for work. It had been delivered that morning. The signature captured her eyes — that of Paul Melandes! Disbelief at what he had written being the uppermost of her emotions. He wanted her to meet him when she had finished work on the following Wednesday. He would be waiting for her from three o'clock at the top of the steps by the sea wall on the pier leading to Castle Cornet. What sort of a monster was he? Bringing another woman into the hotel only the night before and then sending a note asking that she, Sorelle, meet him. He must think she was a fool.

And yet even as she stared at the letter the signature seemed to dissolve and reform into his dark handsome face with its deep probing gaze defying her to refuse to meet him again. The tone of the message had hardly been requesting — more confident expectation that she would be there on the day. She put the letter into the pocket of her blouse, over her breast, as if by doing so she would feel the caress again on it of the hand that had penned the words.

In bed that night she wrestled with the voice of reason and won. Where Paul was concerned she was weak and knew it, excusing this weakness by telling herself that she had refused to communicate with him after he had sent her the flowers, and that it was he who had now got in touch with her again. But the thought of the woman he had escorted the other night still rankled and Sorelle found herself wondering if she would after all have been more sensible to end the affair with Paul permanently. Never had she met such a perplexing, magnetic, hurtful man and yet the thought that she might see him again caused a storm of glorious sensations to burst inside her. She slept with the letter under her pillow.

Half-past three on Wednesday found Sorelle making her way on the upper walk towards Castle Cornet. It was a warm mellow early September afternoon. She had changed her clothes at the hotel and was wearing white lightweight trousers, a blue-and-white-hooped short-sleeved top and a navy blue guernsey carried over her arm — it could become cooler later on.

Down to her left and reached by steps placed at intervals was the road to the castle lined with parked cars and thronged with people. Yachts on cradles being painted or repaired, and the shining oval of the model yacht pond. She was conscious of none of this, only of seeking impatiently for signs of the figure of Paul. Her feet were beginning to catch up with the rhythm of her heart. But she mustn't appear too eager, she told herself. And what would she say to him? This time she must keep her cool, try to forget that it was barely two days ago since he had walked past her with another woman on his arm.

Sorelle saw him first, leaning back against the wall in a relaxed way, arms folded. Then he turned his head in her direction, gave a short wave and watched her approach. In turn she was aware of his tall, figure in a dark blue tee shirt and shorts hugging his brown muscular thighs.

'Nice to see you, Sorelle.' Grey green was uppermost in his changeable hazel eyes smiling warmly at her in welcome, an expression so different from that disastrous evening the last time they had been alone together.

'I didn't finish until three,' she said a trifle awkwardly, and more for something to say than giving an explanation for being late. It was as if they were meeting for the first time.

'I guessed that. I was just admiring your island, it becomes more beautiful each time I see it.'

She followed his glance, seeing the town buildings rising in tiers into the blue. Elizabeth College outlined in the distance and the harbour below vital and bustling. Nearer at hand the green of the Fort George headland and below it the *Privateer*, white in the sparkling placid blue of Havelet Bay. It was beautiful indeed.

Her gaze returned to her companion to find his eyes upon her. Taking her guernsey from her he said, 'I'll go first — the tender's down here.' Sorelle followed and he handed her down the last few steps and into the boat. As he settled beside her he returned the garment smiling. 'A genuine guernsey and a genuine Guernsey girl.' The engine roared into life, the boat turned and began to move quickly away. Any awkwardness that Sorelle had felt was now dispelling fast. Paul Melandes was a master at making a woman feel that she was the only one that mattered. It was as she well knew one of his many charms. It could also be a dangerous and hurtful one.

Once on board Paul led her straight into the saloon where Carlos was waiting, the latter's face expressing a quiet pleasure on meeting Sorelle again.

'A drink for Miss Dalby, Carlos.' His eyes challenged hers. 'If I remember correctly it will be a cinzano with ice and plenty of lemonade. And a sherry for me.'

Sorelle nodded, smiling. Their quarrel seemed never to have happened. Like a film taking the bad parts out and rejoining the remainder.

As Carlos disappeared Paul said, 'I want to show you the island that I bought recently — you'll probably have seen something about it in the papers.'

If only he knew the tempestuous emotions that that report had aroused in her. 'Yes I did. I know of Ormer Island, but I've never actually been on it. There's a legend that it used to be a look-out for pirates preying on shipping round the islands.'

Paul's eyes gleamed. 'Well I don't think that I shall be preying on the shipping.'

It crossed Sorelle's mind that he could instead continue to plunder the hearts of women as he had done hers already.

After Carlos had brought the drinks Paul made a toast, his eyes holding hers, 'To our renewed friendship.' To which Sorelle agreed whole-heartedly. Their meeting had progressed far more easily than she had anticipated.

He glanced after the retreating form of Carlos. 'Carlos was pleased that you were coming, and so was I.'

It flashed across her mind that he must have been confident that she would come — confident enough to inform Carlos.

'You have a way with men, Sorelle, it's quite obvious.' Was he mocking her gently? 'He's quite wise in his judgement of women.'

No doubt that's because he's had a

chance to learn from his time with you, thought Sorelle. 'And I respect his advice,' Paul added.

'Oh, and what was it concerning me?' Sorelle surprised herself with her boldness.

'Ah,' drawled Paul, devilish lights dancing in his eyes. 'It was that I should make haste like hell and get you back here.'

Sorelle smiled broadly with pleasure, her summer blue eyes glowing in the flush of her fair skin. If it were true, good for Carlos. Aloud she said, 'And now I'm here.'

'Yes, you are.' His expression had become serious. He hesitated, and she thought for a moment that he was going to add something else.

'As a grown woman I should have known better, Paul,' she said softly, and seeing immediately that he understood.

'No.' He gave an almost imperceptible shake of his dark head. Suddenly his manner changed, became light and bantering. 'See what happens when a woman comes aboard — I forget things.'

Puzzled, she watched him move across the saloon with an easy animal-like grace. She suddenly had an almost overpowering impulse to run after him, throw herself on her knees and wrap her arms around his hard rippling thighs and kiss them. She realised again that this man had the ability to shatter a woman's common sense.

To her surprise he produced a bunch of roses. Gave them to her with a flourish and a wry smile. 'I meant to give them to you as soon as you came aboard.' He stared deeply into her face. 'You can't refuse them now — you could but I've delivered them anyway. I know you've got them.' She knew he was alluding to the other flowers he had sent to her, and her ignoring of his attempts to renew their friendship.

Sorelle stood up, flowers between herself and Paul. They did not take the hurt of his earlier words away, but they were a peace offering. She reached up and touched his face and planted a kiss upon his warm brown cheek. She had meant it to be just that, but more powerful forces than she could contend with had been set in motion. His lips for some reason became where his cheek had been a moment before, and she moulded willingly in his arms. Everything dissolved into a blur, the roses crushed between them.

A discreet cough interrupted the dream-like state.

'Sorry, Mr. Melandes. You want for me to do anything else?' Carlos asked quaintly.

'I'm taking Miss Dalby to the island, Carlos. Will you prepare a picnic — you know the thing — sandwiches, oh, and tea — Miss Dalby likes tea.' He turned back to Sorelle. 'You haven't eaten yet have you?'

'No, I haven't.' Butterflies filled her stomach instead. How marvellous, they were going to the island.

'That's it then — we'll eat when we get there.'

Sorelle became aware of the roses she

still held, their blooms looking the worse after their crushing. 'Oh, look what I've done to your roses.'

Paul smiled gently and whispered, 'What we've done, you witch.'

'Let me help them,' offered Carlos. 'I see what I can do. In water they become beautiful again.' He seemed eager to be of service to her. She handed the roses to him gratefully.

Paul began to lead her from the saloon towards the after deck. 'We'll cast off in a few minutes, Carlos,' he said over his shoulder. Outside he pointed to steps leading upwards. 'Make yourself comfortable Sorelle on the flying bridge. I'll cast off now.'

She mounted the steps to the platform above with its wheel and large comfortable looking seat. Remembered that was where he had held her in his arms that night and they had danced close together under the stars. Things had gone wrong then — dreadfully wrong.

That was in the past and now they were together again for a while.

She watched Paul below going about the boat making ready to leave. He had a crew she was sure but he seemed to be doing it all himself that afternoon. She felt the gentle swing of the boat's stern and then he appeared over the top of the steps, muscle and sinew outlined in his arms as he pulled himself on to the bridge. He stood at the controls. Pushed a button and she heard the muted roar of engines below, and felt a slight vibration under her feet. Castle Cornet which had been dead ahead of them now appeared to be moving to Sorelle's left as the bows came round and pointed seawards.

Paul glanced at her momentarily, threw her a confidential, contented smile, one which gave her confidence and made her feel that she was part of his life — for that afternoon at least. He slipped sun-glasses on, then pushed a chrome lever forward and the *Privateer* began to move in earnest. His hands caressed the spoke of the polished wooden wheel — hands which had

170

caressed her and brought her to a fever pitch of desire.

She looked back as they began to leave the bay. At the people under the umbrellas outside the café by the road leading towards the aquarium. The parked cars gleaming in the sun. Figures on the cliff path, watching. No doubt they were wondering who she was — who they were on that magnificent yacht. Binoculars trained on them. She had seen it in magazines, travel brochures. The girl on the bridge of the yacht with a handsome man. Now it had happened to her.

Sorelle began to enjoy it. The sun-warmed breeze over the windscreen caressing her, the white gently foaming vee from the bows, the deck stretching ahead and a sensation akin to low flying. In the company of this hand-some, fabulous, wealthy man concentrating serious-faced on the commanding of his boat. And she riding high over a late summer sea with love in her heart.

Outside the shelter of the bay the

wind was cooler. Sorelle shrugged her guernsey on, Paul's hand in the small of her back steadying her. He did not take it away immediately, but just as she looked up at him to acknowledge his help she found his lips meeting hers. But only briefly, he withdrawing self-reprovingly. 'I must concentrate, otherwise I shall run on to Sark, big as it is.' Sorelle hardly cared. This was paradise — a tantalising glimpse of a paradise she had thought was lost totally.

'Apart from that,' Paul added, 'I shall have to be careful that I don't make her jealous.'

Just for a moment Sorelle's happiness waned. She tried to keep her voice light and carefree. 'Oh, I didn't know you dated two on the same day. Is she aboard?'

'She is — all of her.' He tapped the wheel. 'This beauty — the Privateer.' Sorelle laughed, all her happiness flooding back and she observed the wicked tilt to the corners of his lips.

To her left the Fermain ferry was approaching and she looked back to see it roll in the *Privateer's* wake. Above it the buildings rose from the esplanade. She recognised Le Maison Hugo. The attic where she and Paul had stood together, and on whose stairs afterwards she had fallen literally into his arms — their first kiss. It seemed a long time ago now.

Turning seawards again she could see Herm and the yellow strip of its nearest beach. The famous Shell beach was over the other side, she knew. The dark mass of Sark on her right in the distance. Motor boats like small beetles with white tails skimmed the sea, and the occasional sailing yacht slipped by more sedately. Across the harbour the derricks of White Rock Pier stood waiting for the arrival of the afternoon mail boat from the mainland.

Paul stepped back from the wheel, one hand still lightly resting on it. 'Your turn to be helmsman, Sorelle.'

She got in front of him, took the spokes gingerly, nervously. Just a slight tremor like a weak electric current ran through her hands. The wheel was easier to move than she had expected.

Such a great yacht controlled from that small wheel. They seemed to be heading straight for Jethou, near which was Ormer Island.

'Carry on, you're doing just fine,' he murmured into her ear. His hands slipped either side of her body to correct the yacht's direction — large brown masculine hands atop her small soft ones. His hands had tightened over hers. Then they folded round her waist, his lips nuzzling at her neck. It was a marvellous dream from which she did not wish to awake.

'It's fabulous, but you take over Paul — I feel safer.' She'd enjoyed the feeling of being one with the boat but she hadn't been able to concentrate. The bridge of the *Privateer* between islands was no place in which to allow her passions to become inflamed, nor his for that matter. She moved sideways reluctantly.

'All right,' he breathed huskily, 'I'll

take command again.' You were in command of me, she thought.

Soon they were passing Jethou — small, high out of the water, barren looking from a distance. Sorelle knew that it too was privately owned. Beyond it she could see the island that Paul had bought — Ormer Island, about a mile past Jethou and off the southern tip of Herm. As far as she knew no boat trips from Guernsey had ever been arranged to take holiday-makers there as there were to the other islands. She knew that it had been occupied once in the fifties and that it had been uninhabited since. A place somewhat shrouded in mystery.

She glanced at the man by her side who was shortly going to show it to her, couldn't quite get used to the fact of someone buying an island — a whole island. A house yes, or land, but an island . . .

As they neared it Sorelle saw that it appeared to be well wooded, the trees growing almost to the edge of the low southern cliffs. A small stretch of golden beach broke this shoreline. Off the nearer western end she could see a small jetty, and behind it the sandy foreshore rose gradually to a fringe of trees beyond which she could not see.

Paul anchored the *Privateer* about two hundred yards out then gave orders to Carlos to take Sorelle and himself ashore. 'Now you shall see my fairy-tale island, Sorelle,' he announced. She discerned a note of barely suppressed excitement. His attaining ownership of the island obviously meant a great deal to him.

7

As Carlos departed back to the *Privateer* Paul took Sorelle's hand and they walked along the old wooden jetty past a small launch tied there, then on to Ormer Island. He led her up a curving gently climbing path towards the fringe of trees she had seen from the yacht.

'Have you ever been to this island before, Sorelle?' His question surprised her.

'No, I haven't. I've been to the others but never this one. Nobody ever suggested it. And they didn't run trips here. Perhaps it was too quiet — no shops or anything.'

'This is my third visit,' he informed her. 'Apart from Carlos and workmen you're the only person — the only woman to come here since I bought it.'

'I'm honoured, Paul,' she smiled up

at him. Indeed she must be. Nice to know she was the first woman — provided that he was telling the truth. Hoped desperately that she'd be the last and only one. He had obviously not thought it worth while bringing the dark-haired woman who had been with him in the hotel restaurant the other night.

She sighed inwardly. If only a miracle would occur and he would say that he loved her and that he had brought her to view their future home together. Oh, if only . . . But that was never likely to happen. He was not, as she knew now, a man who indulged in talk of marriage with any woman. She must enjoy the day in his company and keep a shield around her vulnerable heart — vulnerable as far as the man beside her was concerned.

They paused as the path levelled off at the line of trees, Sorelle welcoming the latter's shade. Paul drew her to his side and pointed ahead. 'There it is — Ormer House,' he announced with a

178

quiet proud satisfaction.

Sorelle gasped. About two hundred yards away and slightly below them was a house set in a miniature valley. The path they had come up continued down from the line of trees towards it. The building was set end on to where they stood and she could make out level cleared areas around as much of the house as she could see. Trees seemed to ring the island like a natural fence, except for a gap on the southern side, the yellow crescent revealing the beach she had seen from the yacht. 'Oh, it's marvellous, Paul. How peaceful.'

'It isn't when you get near. I've got workmen in.'

'They're in now?'

'Yes, I want the place to be ready for occupation as soon as possible. I can't wait to get in.'

She wasn't surprised at that. It was a heavenly spot. 'And it's all yours,' she said dreamily, wonderingly. 'The whole place, the island — the lot?'

Paul studied her a moment. 'Do I

hear a note of disapproval. Don't you agree with one person owning it all?'

Just in time Sorelle saw the provocative gleam in his expressive eyes. In the shade under the trees they looked more grey. 'No, you don't Mr Paul Melandes. I approve of it very much,' she answered lightly. 'You've worked hard no doubt to be able to buy what you want. It's a beautiful place and I'm sure when you've done everything with it, it will be even more beautiful. You haven't taken anyone's house away, you're improving what was already here and that must be good. I'm very pleased for you.'

Paul's arm tightened round her middle. 'You're an articulate little thing when you get going, Miss Dalby.' Jerked his head at the house. 'Want to see it?'

'Oh yes, I do.' Her enthusiasm was real. They set off down the path, he keeping her drawn close to him. It was a sheer sensual pleasure for her, their thighs moving one upon the other in step.

Reaching the house Sorelle realised that it was a lot larger than it had appeared from a distance. It was typical of the older type of Guernsey building, made of thick solid granite. The sounds of work being done filtered through to her. A huge window at the far end, half the height of the building and yards in length dazzled her with its reflection of the sun.

'That's the indoor swimming pool behind there,' Paul informed her in answer to her curiosity. 'The window will slide open for when it's warm.' He indicated a flat patch of ground in front of the window. 'The outdoor pool will be there, but that won't be finished till next year.' Pointed to a wide strip of newly laid green paving in front of the window. 'That's going to be the terracing, and I think I shall have some of the trees taken down — I like trees but they can make a house dark inside.'

She could see where the garden had been once, but now it was overgrown and unkempt. Paul saw her looking.

'When they're finished inside, I'll get them to straighten and landscape that area.'

Sorelle's eyes followed the path from the house down between bushes to the sandy cove. 'It's beautiful, Paul,' she said turning back to him to find him watching her.

'Are you any good at gardening, Sorelle?' A simple everyday question but he was eyeing her closely.

She smiled. 'I like flowers and plants, and I once did a course in flower arranging but that's a bit different I suppose.'

'It's a start.' He smiled into her face. 'I'll engage you right away.' Oh, if only he would. She'd do anything, If only he'd say he loved her.

'Come on, I'll show you inside,' he said taking her by the hand.

The sturdy hard exterior of the house belied the growing luxury of its interior. Distinctive furniture, and the very latest in kitchens. A bathroom — all marble and gold, a place in which she could spend the day relaxing. The special arched fire-place where no doubt in the winter a roaring log fire would cast its warming cheerful shadows around. Money had obviously been no object, but like Paul's quarters on the yacht, it needed brightening, being sombre in its colouring.

Just as she was about to follow Paul into the sunshine again, her eyes were caught by the glint of an ashtray. Sorelle's gaze riveted on the remains of a cigarette in it. Not stubbed out hard but half smoked as if someone had placed it there and forgotten about it. There was lipstick on the end. Her mind rushed to find excuses for it being there — to ease the hurtful shock she felt. Workmen were in the house but they did not wear lipstick. What about a woman — a daily help? It could be, but as he was not yet living there it seemed unlikely. Had Margot been there, or Ann? But he had told her she was the first woman that he had taken to the island. He had lied — of that she was now certain.

The workmen were beginning to leave as she and Paul made their way outside again. 'Well, does it meet with your approval, Sorelle?' There was a smile in his eyes but also a deep thoughtfulness.

'It's fabulous, Paul, and I'm sure you're going to like it here.' She wished she had never gone into the house now.

'D'you think it needs a woman?'

How could he ask her that when one had been there already? She was surprised at his glibness — his nerve, and hesitated over her answer, afraid that her real feelings would show through. 'I — I suppose so. What do they say — a woman's touch, although I think you've done all right yourself.' She was aware again of his searching regard of her as if he were filing things away in his mind. Had caught him observing her before in the house. It made her slightly uncomfortable.

He nodded, looked away. 'Yes, I'll

have to get some help in.' Glanced at her again. 'Perhaps you might know of someone.'

Indeed she did — herself, but she would not share him with others. 'I'll ask around,' she said carelessly. Inwardly she sighed sadly as she gazed at the house. She would never be mistress of it.

Perhaps she was the first of a long line that would visit the house, each thinking that she was the one he was going to give his heart to. They would find out as she had done that he was a charming, sexually formidable man, able to sweep a woman off her feet on short acquaintance. But the ride to paradise was short-lived — the return to earth brutally hard.

Paul picked up the picnic basket, then took hold of her arm, his voice interrupting her thoughts, low and caressing her ear like the murmur of the sea that lovely day. 'Come along, I'm beginning to feel hungry. We'll eat down on the beach. It's the only one on the island so I shall never have to decide which one I'm going to visit — it simplifies things.'

But things for her were becoming more complicated and some of her former happiness of that afternoon had gone after noticing that cigarette with lipstick on it. She steeled herself, tried to make herself accept this man as he was. The alternative was to get out of his life. Her mind rebelled at the idea — she was hopelessly in love with him.

They walked down the path to the beach between large rhododendron bushes, and bluebells nodded in the warm breeze below them. If only they were married and lived in Ormer House, just taking a stroll together. He had just told her he loved her for the hundredth time that day.

The trees fringing the island gave way on either side of the small beach, and grass carpeted the few yards of sloping low cliffs in front of them. The northern coast of Sark lay dark green in the hazy heat of the afternoon, and away to the left she thought she could just discern the French coast. How beautiful and peaceful it was. Just she and Paul, and the gulls — their plaintive cry echoing the plea from her heart to be loved by the man at her side.

Slipping her sandals off she felt the warmth of the soft white sand as she walked on the empty beach. Paul selected a spot halfway down then opened the basket. Carlos had done a good job, thought Sorelle, as they dined.

Afterwards Sorelle lay down and stretched luxuriously, enjoying the sensuous thrill of knowing that his eyes were raking her body. Turning to face him she said, 'D'you think that you'll ever be lonely here?' Straightaway she wished she had not asked the question. He would think she was fishing for another invitation. Just for a moment she glimpsed a strange sad look before he glanced away thoughtfully. It had gone when he regarded her again.

'Well I shall not be home each day because I'll be away on business sometimes, though I shall try of course to spend as much time as possible here. As a matter of fact I'm thinking of selling some of my holdings in the States — concentrating more on the European side of things.'

Oh please concentrate on me too, she prayed silently. At least he would be nearer — Europe didn't seem as far away as America.

'And a lot of my contacts on the Continent can be reached in a few hours from here.' Paul pointed behind him vaguely. 'That's why I'm having a helicopter pad built over there. The *Privateer* would be too slow.' He smiled at her, his eyes suddenly glowing with enthusiasm. 'This is a dream come true for me, Sorelle. I always wanted an island of my own.'

You get most things you want, she thought. Suddenly jealously seized her, of something that could bring such a light to his eyes.

Paul pulled off his tee-shirt, and she observed the rippling hard muscles on his shoulders and arms highlighted by the gleam of sweat. He turned towards her, leaning on his elbow, the black dense curls of chest hair hiding the flesh almost completely, and gave a definite shake of his head. 'No, I'm certainly not going to be lonely.' His eyes looked sea green now and trained into hers. 'You'll be here. I want to see you again.'

Yes, she thought with some bitterness. Drop in on her, phone her. She'd be there waiting, then afterwards off he'd go to someone else. Very convenient for him. It would be heartbreaking to know that he would be living at times so near to her, and yet in a way so distant from her. Sorelle sat up clasping her legs, the frustration and hopelessness in her mind over her companion making her body restless. Just around the edge of the low cliff she could see the stern of the *Privateer*, white and shining.

Paul raised himself beside her, must have guessed she was gazing at the yacht. 'I may get rid of the *Privateer*.'

'Oh no — I . . . ' The utterance sprang from her. Glanced at him, looked away in some confusion. 'I mean . . . '

'You like it don't you?'

'Yes — yes I do, though I know it's nothing to do with me.' She did like the yacht — it meant a great deal to her. Although they had quarrelled on it, the *Privateer* was the great white sea horse that had brought the man she loved — her prince into her life. Whether he would ever be her prince of love was doubtful.

'The only reason that made me think about selling,' Paul said, 'was that there isn't enough shelter here. In winter she could get blown on to the rocks if she were to be anchored off the island.' He paused thoughtfully, eyes narrowed. 'I don't want to sell her,' he admitted.

'You could keep it in the marina at Saint Peter Port. It would be safe enough there I'm sure,' Sorelle suggested.

'That's an idea, I think it would,' he agreed, 'or,' he leaned towards her serious-faced, 'I could give it to you for an early Christmas present. How would you like that?'

She saw the teasing humour rising in the hazel eyes, chuckled at him as his lips gave way into the slow reluctant smile that was one of his characteristics. 'No doubt the first time out I should run it on to the rocks.'

'I should have to give you some lessons first — but it's not so difficult.'

'Oh, I'm sure it is.'

'All right, you can have the *Privateer* when you can handle it. I shall instruct you, take you on a course round the islands.'

His gaze locked onto and held her own.

She was quite sure that he was the kind of man who could make a present of a yacht as if it were a box of chocolates. If only though she could tell him of the fierce yearning in her for his love, and her burning desire to give hers to him. Yachts, houses, cars and islands were insignificant beside that. He was the sun around which her life had begun to revolve.

His gaze shifted, moving appraisingly over the rest of her. Then his eyes rose to meet hers again, admiration in them. 'You know something Sorelle, I might even decide to call this beach after you — Sorelle's beach.' He gave a satisfied nod. 'Sounds good — I like it.'

She looked at him from under suddenly heavy eyelids with a mounting desire — 'And what will the price be for such a great honour, sir?' Her voice was tremulous when she spoke. He must hear it and see it. Wanted to feel his hands taking possession of her.

In one easy movement he was kneeling at her side, above her, lips hovering close to hers, his body gently coaxing hers to the sand. 'A kiss, Miss Dalby,' he breathed huskily, half banteringly, but his swiftly darkening, glazed and half closed eyes told of a desire that had overtaken him also. Kissed her on the mouth briefly, lightly, torturingly. 'This has been the most wonderful day of my life, Sorelle, alone on this island with you. All these years that I've wasted, dearest Sorelle, when I could have known you. Sorelle — oh Sorelle.' His kisses fell on her eyes, her throat. The words thrilled her, but she was hungry for the sound of his voice saying he loved her.

Then his lips descended savagely on hers, his upper body crushing her into the moulding sand, his maleness and virility beating down in waves upon her — swamping her senses until that was all she was aware of. The pressure of his mouth was relentless like an incoming tide. His tongue had become a spear thrusting aside her lips to dominate hers, and his thighs were hard upon hers. His hand stroked her cheek, the side of her throat, then it became seeking, unbuttoning the top of her blouse, exploring tenderly the softness of her breasts below, and paving the way for his lips. His fingers caressed the length of her spine urgently, pressing her ever closer.

She was on fire, inwardly screaming eagerly for him not to refrain from touching every part, conscious of her wantonness, but unable and unwilling on this occasion to halt the surge of desire. His lips returned to her mouth again, but she pulled his head down deep into her breasts, her fingers curled to make loving furrows through his hair. The sky had gone, Paul blotting it out. Sorelle lost track of time.

Suddenly Paul moved his head. She heard him swear. Something wet and cold touched her feet. His weight left her and she blinked in the light, sat up dull-eyed. The tide had reached them reminding them of the world around. Anger and amusement vied for command in Paul's face. He swore at the sea then looked at her and they laughed together wryly. He helped her to her feet, a wicked glint showing through the glaze of his desire. 'Come along Sorelle, the sea says 'no' this time.' His throat sounded dry. 'I'll show you the rest of the island.'

She had a feeling that he was slightly relieved at the intervention of the tide in their love-making. Was it, she wondered, because he had revealed more of his true feelings in his passion than he had intended? He was certainly not the man to pass up the chance of making total love to a woman. She glanced back to where they had lain. Saw the sand churned by their feet, the hollowing by their bodies. The water covering the marks of passion — soon to be obliterated. Would those feelings he had just expressed to her a few minutes ago be obliterated by time also?

Her head rested against the muscular wall of his chest as they followed the path in sight of the sea. Shade from the trees dappled the way, their trunks black against the azure of the late afternoon sky. The island was an Eden for she and Paul to be alone on. She stole a glance up at him. He looked thoughtful with a determined line to his jaw. Was he thinking as she had done of what would have happened if the sea had not interrupted their love-making? Perhaps he was making plans so that the next time it would be different.

He had not said 'I love you', but was she right in thinking that love had been in those powerful hands used so lightly? His kisses, the strokes of his fingers that had set her pulse near to explosion point. In his voice — his words. She remembered what he had said. The most wonderful day of his life — a man who must have had many wonderful days in his life of one sort or another. Didn't all this tell of his love for her? Would he say so in words before long? A voice inside hissed at her to ask him there and then whether he loved her or not. Now! Go on! Sorelle recoiled from the act. Could not face the risk of his reply bringing heartbreak. Rather she go on living in a make-believe land that it would happen soon and she would hear the magic words.

They reached the far end of the small island and Paul pointed at a circular patch where the ground had been levelled and trees cleared. 'That's going to be the helicopter pad. Be in Guernsey Airport in no time, or Jersey for that matter. Have you ever been up in one?' She hadn't. 'Well, as soon as it's all set up I'll bring it over and pick you up at the airport. You can help me do some shopping, then we'll fly back here. How's that?'

'That would be marvellous,' she told him, eyes glowing. How easy he made it all sound, so wonderful. He endowed everything with a touch of adventure. She felt caught up and living when she was with him.

They proceeded back in the direction of the house, her fingers entwined in his in a happy silence. Happy until they reached the house again, where she was immediately reminded of the cigarette with the lipstick upon it. The memory clouded the golden afternoon. He had lied to her deliberately. It wasn't an oversight on his part — you just didn't forget things like that.

The object of her thoughts was busy shrugging his tee top on again. Her eyes strayed to his satin sheened tanned body in the moment his face was hidden. Rippling with the power to crush her and love her again completely — if he wished next time. Next time . . . Their eyes met and she smiled cheerfully to hide her misgivings for the future.

Back on board the *Privateer* they were served a meal by Carlos. Paul smiled over his plate at her, a mischievous light in his eyes. 'Carlos has set the cockles and tomatoes in your honour as a tribute to Guernsey, from the sea — from the land. I told him Guernsey tomatoes were considered the best.' His voice deepened further, his look provocative. 'I want you to have some onions also then I shall not offend you later.'

Was he thinking of kissing her later? Would he carry on where he had left off that afternoon? If only he would say he loved her first and then she would give herself to him willingly.

Afterwards he opened a bottle of champagne. They touched glasses. 'Here's to you and Ormer Island.'

'Thanks Paul — to Ormer Island. It was wonderful for me — a great afternoon.' It had been, yet heart breaking in the uncertainty which constantly pervaded her when she was with him. But at least he had put her first in the order of his toast.

Then they danced to records, and Sorelle was surprised that he did not attempt to make love to her again. He kissed her occasionally as they swayed close together. The ardour was present in his lips but he did not allow himself to be carried away by his desire. There was obviously to be no repetition of that other night which ended up with her making that scene. She was glad of the subdued lighting as she coloured at the memory of the way in which she had behaved then.

Later Carlos brought them coffee up on deck and Sorelle in the gathering darkness pointed out places of interest along the waterfront to Paul. She was aware of a subtle difference in his attitude towards her from the last time she had been on board — in fact from the last time she had seen him. The dominating challenge was still there in his eyes but she realised during the evening that he had drawn her to speak about herself and her family, and her wider interests without her being aware of it. He had revealed another side of his nature to her — a warm caring one interested in another human being's problems with the world about.

The town clock struck ten as they gazed across the water. She must not outstay her welcome — must leave soon, frightened that something would break the spell she was under in the company of Paul Melandes. Like Cinderella she must go home before that happened and prepare for ordinary life to begin again the following morning. She was just about to tell him when he spoke without looking at her.

'What d'you want from life in the

future, Sorelle?' She was quite unprepared for his question voiced so seriously, and gazed at his profile dimly illuminated by the yacht's deck lights. He glanced at her quickly as if impatient for her answer, then away again.

You — you — you, she wanted to shout. That's what I want — nothing more. Gathered her thoughts into something rational to say. Said slowly, 'Happiness, and I want to be able to know when I've got that happiness — recognise it.' She paused then added wistfully and reflectively, 'Some happiness comes and goes so quickly, you hardly know it's been until you look back.' She went on, 'Children if possible, a nice home and my mother and family to keep well.' She smiled at him, shrugged, 'I think that's all. I'd better not ask for too much, otherwise whoever it is looking after me may think me greedy.'

Paul turned to her, shadows cutting across his face. 'That doesn't say much for the men of this world,' and his voice held a wry mocking quality. 'You've forgotten to mention what I would have thought quite important — a man. Was it deliberate?'

Please don't tease me, she thought — it hurts. If only you could love me then I could tell you of the man I love — you. Steadied her breathing. 'Happiness would be the man I love. That's what I want.' She sighed. 'I've discovered that I'm a one-man girl. Just saving myself for Mr Right when he comes along.'

Something like pain flickered across her companion's features and he frowned. 'Obviously Mr Right as you talk about hasn't appeared yet. You may have to settle for second best. Maybe your standards are too high.'

Oh, if only he realised. She couldn't see his full expression, just reflected pinpoints of light in the shadows of his eyes as he continued to stare at her.

The *Privateer* moved beneath them, her lights dancing in the water. Muted music floated from somewhere in the inner harbour, out of the patchwork of coloured cabin curtains, along with the jingling of the sailing boats' shrouds plucked by the breeze.

'Do you like second best in anything, Paul?' Sorelle countered gently. They had shared glorious hours together and she did not want to say anything to spoil the memory. She was relieved when he chuckled.

'No, Miss Guernsey. You're right — no I don't.' His arm encircled her waist, his cheek touching her hair. 'And you're definitely not second best,' the deeply whispered tones caressing her innermost nerves like a bow played lovingly upon a violin.

'I think I shall have to be leaving soon, Paul,' she murmured weakly, reluctantly.

'Let Carlos make you a coffee before you go, Sorelle,' Paul said guiding her persuasively between the doors into the saloon.

Afterwards they stood in each other's arms and out of sight of Carlos waiting in the boat below to take her back to the jetty. Paul kissed her the pressure of his lips holding a fierceness — a longing — but one which he had under control. At last he pushed her away from him gently and stroked her hair with the palm of his hand — a tender action. 'My Sorelle.' His voice was tight with some emotion. 'I'll call you.' He turned away as if the effort of restraining such an emotion was almost too much for him.

She turned and waved as the boat left the *Privateer's* side, and Paul returned it. Perhaps she was tired and her own emotions unsteady from that last embrace, but she couldn't help the thought that maybe it was from him a wave of farewell. The end of a shipboard romance — an unfulfilled one. A subject of conjecture in the years ahead as to what might have been for her.

Carlos saw her into the taxi that Paul had ordered. What a nice man, she thought. He too must be tired and had played his part in making it a lovely day for her. She had caught his look of admiration when she had got into the boat. He was not a young man and she looked at him with some concern. 'Thank you, Carlos. Now you must get some rest. You've worked hard for us today. Go straight to bed.'

He shrugged and smiled a tolerant understanding smile. 'I get rest. Don't worry. Mr Melandes good boss — tough, expect good work. But he good to me.' He looked around him conspiratorily, a twinkle from the stars in his eyes. 'I tell you he likes you.' He nodded knowingly and stood back as the taxi moved off.

Sorelle sighed tiredly in the darkness of the cab. Like! Could it ever be love one day?

In bed that night her body wanted sleep but her mind was restless. She had a feeling of anticlimax — of near melancholy. His whispered, 'I'll call you' now seemed to her a polite and kindly way of giving her the brush-off. She had just been a visitor for the afternoon, to see his house, an amusing few hours for him. Perhaps he would think of her with some affection when he flicked the pages of his memory occasionally.

Her spirits sank lower as the incident of the cigarette with lipstick on it loomed large in her mind, overshadowing the real joys of the times they had spent together. There would no doubt be other men in her life. She may even marry, but always she knew she would be waiting for him to call her. She made a great effort to dispel the gloom pervading her thoughts. 'My Sorelle'. Had he not said those words? How wonderful they had sounded. Then mockery stole into her mind. Like the *Privateer*, his business, his house — a belonging. She must not read too much into what he had said in the heat of passion. On the other hand he had been extremely nice to her, bearing no trace of ill-will towards her after the scene she had made on the yacht the time before. Sleep did come but not until she had relived once more the ecstasy in his arms on the beach, the sea denying them so cruelly full knowledge of each other.

8

Paul did call her the next day, and the next, and the one after that. Dizzy heady days for Sorelle wrapped in the joy of his companionship and his increasing and caring attention towards her. How could she have doubted that he would call her? He took her to the very finest restaurants on the island, bought her clothes if she as much as glanced at some delectable concoction of the dressmaker's art. Insisted that she have it. Shop assistants fluttered around her as if she were some world-wide known celebrity.

On the Thursday he hired a plane to fly them over to Jersey where they dined by candlelight, serenaded by a guitarist at a small intimate restaurant with an Italian name just off the harbour at St Aubins. Over the table he had looked deeply and meaningfully into her face, his eyes glowing and smiling, the short strong hair framing the tanned face above the cream lightweight jacket that he wore. Afterwards, and bemused by the magic of Paul's company, she tried hard to remember the restaurant's name, for it was there that she realised beyond any doubt that he was the one man she would love to her life's end.

Now it was another day and Sorelle was trying to cope with the normal routine of her work again. Was it only yesterday that they were on that long curving beach where they had first waded then splashed through the low waves? Their kisses at intervals along the white golden crescent, the water dripping from the hairs of his chest on to her breasts during their embraces, and the September sun drying them with its gentle heat.

He had said that he would get in touch with her on Saturday. Her life would fall apart if he did not. The man was like a drug circulating in her blood-stream — she couldn't do without him. All at once her work behind the reception desk had become tedious and her enthusiasm had waned. A few days drifting along on cloud nine with a rich handsome man had sapped her ability to live in the real world — one where she had to earn a living.

Sorelle was glad when she could go home to the comforting surroundings of her small flat. Once there she made herself a cup of tea and switched on the television. The main news was just ending and the island news beginning. She watched idly as a couple of men talked about the increase in visitors to Guernsey that summer. Sorelle sighed gently. It didn't seem long since the spring, now sadly it was drawing near the end of September and the daylight a little shorter. Glancing outside her window she saw the changing colours of the trees in the late afternoon shade.

A name drifted across the room from the television, nudging her mind. It came again, making her fully aware — suddenly on the edge of her seat wide-eyed in surprise. Paul was being interviewed. The serious face with curled corners to the mouth. She was conscious of the house in the background. Recognised it — it was the one on Ormer Island.

The interviewer was saying, 'This summer Mr Melandes came to our island and liked what he saw and decided to buy a smaller edition of it — Ormer Island. Behind me is the house that goes with the island, and which Mr Melandes has refurbished.' He turned to Paul as Sorelle watched fixedly. 'Can you tell us whether you have any further plans Mr Melandes for the house?'

Paul's face was in close up as he replied, 'I shall live here between business trips. It is an ideal place as a base from which I can manage and build up my company's trading in Europe. In my short while here I've come to like the islands very much — Guernsey in particular. If the company continues to do as well in Europe as it has done so far, and I see no reason why it shouldn't, then most probably I shall settle here — it depends.' Sorelle watched his slow smile, the half shrug, and saw clearly the lips that had fastened on hers in passion. His deep-set eyes regarded her unseeing from the screen. Her legs had become jelly, her tea forgotten. This must have been the business that he had said he had that day. Possibly filmed that morning, she thought. She could see figures in the background, probably workmen still engaged on the house.

The interviewer then asked a question which was like a spear poised to enter Sorelle's heart as she waited for what she might hear. 'Is Mrs Melandes in the islands with you?'

She saw Paul's eyes narrow and harden momentarily but then an affable and impish humour appeared swiftly as he stated quietly, 'There is no Mrs Melandes.' He paused a moment — 'yet.' Vast relief flooded through Sorelle. Paul went on, 'But I have plans to marry in the future,' and half turned his head away indicating his wish for an end to the interview. But the other persisted 'Would you bring your bride to live here, Mr Melandes?'

'Of course, it would be my home and hers.' An impatience showed in his expression and tone.

'Thank you, Mr Melandes.'

The picture faded leaving Sorelle staring trance-like at the set, unheeding of the following programme. Plans to marry! Who? Almost every girl in the island would give anything to become Mrs Melandes, she guessed. Had he anyone in mind? If only it could be herself he was thinking of. All that evening she swung between a wild and fearful hope and deep despair, balancing the pros and cons in her mind.

She and Paul had been together a number of times, he appearing to enjoy her company after their first quarrel — which was now past. He had whispered endearments to her, treated her well and generously. Had taken her to see his house to which he had just said he would bring his bride. And his passion on the beach had been strong enough to melt any resistance she might have felt. On the other hand he had never said anything which could be construed to mean that he loved her. Those three words had yet to be spoken by him. Even his tender sayings had been on the rushing wings of desire. He could have uttered them to any woman. And she herself had seen another less pleasant side to him earlier in their acquaintanceship. He had told her not to look for marriage with him. That had been on the *Privateer* that night. He had thought she was a good time girl. Did he think any different of her now?

And could his talk of marriage be a further extension of the game he was said to have played with the women in his life, since he had been deserted on his wedding day? A cruel refinement of the game, and the let down all the more hard for the naïve hopefuls. All right if you knew the rules and played to them.

Sorelle smiled wryly. She was the girl who had decided to play it cool. Now look at her.

The following day after work Sorelle decided to do some shopping, and at the same time get a birthday card for her brother. She found a card, posted it and then walked down High Street towards the town church — the latter's clock showing nearly half past three, and on to the esplanade.

She decided to go into Ambrosios — have a coffee and unwind in the process. There was a table free at the side of the doorway from which she could see out. Passers-by, the boats, the sky — a moving changing picture framed by the open front of the premises. Another month and it would be much quieter. She tried to empty her mind and not to think of Paul. Two people — a man and a woman appeared in Sorelle's line of sight and were gone in seconds. But her eyes had captured them, they becoming a snapshot in her memory. The woman in green, red-haired, fashionable, Margot! The man with her was Paul.

Sorelle stared down into her cup in shocked and hurt surprise. Wished she could banish the picture from her mind. It was vivid, tormenting. Margot looking up at Paul with an air of easy familiarity, her hands round his arm gliding along with the well-practised walk of a model. Her expression had been one of well-satisfied contentment. What had Paul said or done to bring that expression to Margot's face, wondered Sorelle miserably? Hell! Why had she to see them?

Later she collected her car from the hotel car-park and drove home, seeing little of what was going on around her, her thoughts on the man who unknowingly had hurt her again. No wonder he hadn't called her, he was too busy taking Margot out. Where had they been? No doubt he had taken her to lunch. And where were they going? To the yacht? Or to the island? Could that have been Margot's cigarette in the house that day? Was she the bride he had in mind to settle down with on Ormer Island? She had been after him for a long time. Sorelle stared out through misty eyes. Perhaps they were more suited for each other, both being sophisticated people.

Back in the flat she slumped into her chair brooding. Paul had once told her that he and Margot were just good friends — business friends. Sorelle sighed angrily. The flash of anger became a righteous jealousy. Paul had occupied her mind, her feelings, and almost her body. Only unforeseen circumstances had prevented him from possessing her fully, as on the beach at Ormer Island when the tide had interrupted their love-making. She was all too aware of the passions he had aroused in her, and he had no right to play around elsewhere. Why couldn't he have told her he did not want to see her any more? One savage hurt and it would be over.

She ran a bath, soaked in it. The

emotional storm had taken its toll of her and she felt drained of energy. There was nothing to do but accept that the affair had been good whilst it lasted. She laughed miserably. She hadn't even the memory of a bed shared together, the feel of his powerful athletic body possessing her.

It was with an effort that she arose for work in the morning. The early sky was grey and overcast, reflecting her own mood. When she arrived the night porter told her there was a message for her on the desk. It had come in the day before. Even before she saw the signature, she recognised the special notepaper from the yacht. The paper trembled in her fingers in time to the thud of her quickened heart-beats. It was from Paul! He would be taking her out to dinner and would call for her at the flat at nine that evening, Saturday September the twenty-first.

Suddenly all the anxieties and miseries of yesterday were gone. The memory and hurt at the sight of Margot with him fading into insignificance at the relief and joy that he had not forsaken her. She began to find excuses for him. Perhaps it had been something to do with a modelling job that had made it necessary for him to be with Margot. And he really couldn't be blamed for the look on the latter's face. Any woman seen out in Paul Melandes' company would have worn that look. She herself had, she was sure. Yesterday's doubts and fears had been due to tiredness and over-sensitivity. After all he was a bachelor — he had a right to go with whom he pleased. And tonight it was to be her for a few glorious hours.

Paul called for her in a silver Mercedes saloon, and as they drifted away from the curve he smiled sideways at her. 'I thought this might be a little warmer for you than the open car.'

Sorelle returned his smile. Nice of him to think of her like that. Spoke happily at his profile as he drove. 'It's beautiful, Paul.' And so are you she thought, her heart turning over at the sight of him. Easily, comfortably dressed in a fawn suit emphasising the vee-shape of his upper body tapering to lean hips. A brown bow tie with long ends above his white shirt. His handsome and lean muscularity prompted thoughts in her that were more usual towards the end of an evening.

They were soon in town and her companion parked the car outside a restaurant on the esplanade. Sorelle recognised it as being one of the best and also most expensive on the island. Paul must have booked, because the owner and head waiter were waiting to receive them. The place was busy — it being Saturday, but a table by the window and overlooking the marina and harbour had been reserved for them.

She looked out of the window. It was a lovely evening, quiet and still, with dusk's curtain drawing over, softening everything. The mail boat was in and Castle Cornet's lights were coming into their own. Beyond the myriad of masts she thought she could make out Ormer Island. Turning to him again she found him observing her. The same look of admiration was showing as it had been earlier that evening when he had called for her.

'You look delightful — ravishing, Sorelle,' his gaze taking in her dress and his expression telling of his entire satisfaction with what he saw.

The compliment pinked her cheeks. 'Thanks Paul, I'm so glad you like your purchase.' She felt a million dollars in it. The dress was one of the things he had bought her. She had seen it, actually only paused to look at it — it being so far above what she could afford to pay, but he must have noticed her expression, took her in and bought the dress. She had decided to wear it specially for him that night. White and made of a soft jersey wool which hugged and flattered her curves, almost too much she had thought when she had first tried it on. A gold chain encircled her waist, with a matching one round her neck. Two long strips of the same material attached at the shoulders crossed at her throat and fell gracefully down her back. There had been moments yesterday when she was doubtful whether she would ever wear it, and now having worn it, was she herself being bought? Perhaps in the nicest and most civilised way possible. She met his eyes across the table as he poured her drink and the thought crumbled under their compelling gaze.

They chatted easily over the meal, his whole attention focused on her. Even the moments spent ordering the courses he seemed to begrudge.

Over coffee she told him, 'This is a lovely place, Paul. I've never been here before — I'm glad we came.'

His big but not clumsy hands took hers and placed them palm downwards on the table, then gently covered them almost hiding hers. 'Yes, I'm glad too, Sorelle,' he said softly. 'You go with the place — fit the image. You have this ability to look right in any setting.'

She looked for signs that he was teasing her, of insincerity in his face. She found none. He appeared serious. The thought came to her that it was an autumn day. Their affair had blossomed like the spring, but would it flourish and become an evergreen? Or would it shrivel after a short season of hope?

Whatever Paul might have said next was interrupted by the waiter with their liqueurs. He sipped at his then said, 'I suppose you'll know about my interview?'

'I'd heard about it — somebody at the hotel mentioned it,' she replied easily.

'You didn't see it?' His eyes seemed to have the power of wrenching the truth from her.

She resisted and lied, not knowing quite why. Perhaps because she didn't want him to think that she was hanging on to every word and deed of his when she was apart from him. A kind of pride. 'No', she smiled. 'I — I decided to catch up on some shopping that afternoon, and I was rather late getting home. You're a celebrity, you're known now in the island. It's a small place and you give people something to talk about.'

'D'you talk about me?' His eyes challenged hers.

'No.' She shook her head. This time she was truthful.

He studied her quizzically. 'No, I don't think you would.' He went on, 'It's just as well you didn't see the interview. This damned reporter kept asking fool questions.'

'Oh, what about?' she asked carelessly. Would he reveal something of his marriage plans?

'Well he went on about was I going to settle here — I mean on Ormer Island. I said possibly in between business trips.' That was true, thought Sorelle. 'Then the guy asked whether I was bringing Mrs Melandes there.' Paul laughed shortly but she heard no humour in the sound. He shook his head in a gesture of wonder, half shrugged. 'Where do they get these ideas from? There's certainly no Mrs Melandes, that's for sure. Never has been.' He looked straight into Sorelle's face. 'No sir, that's certainly for sure.'

And never will be, Sorelle thought, her heart fluttering weakly like the candles on their table, her feeling of *joie de vivre* that evening suddenly evaporated. 'No, of course not,' she agreed miserably, leaving her eyes on guard and automatically returning the right response to her companion. Her mind was busy. So there she had it. He had implied that the idea of a Mrs Melandes was anathema to him. Straight from the horse's mouth — the stallion's mouth more likely she thought bitterly. He had, she was certain, deliberately said that in such unequivocal tones. It was obviously to warn her off the marriage stakes.

Even so she grasped at straws remembering that during the television interview Paul had said he had plans to marry in the future and would take his bride to live at Ormer House. And so he could agreed a hurtful voice inside her, pointing out that there were other eligible women about besides herself. Margot and the dark-haired woman he'd once brought into the hotel restaurant and probably others she had never seen. She gave a long inward sigh. Her heart was like a yo-yo on the end of Paul's string.

His voice came through to her. 'Are you all right, Sorelle?' Had he seen the torment in her eyes? He was staring at her in serious concern.

She'd meant to say that she was, plead a headache, blame the wine — anything. Instead to the horror of her ordinary self she said, 'No I'm not.' Passed a hand across her forehead in a sudden irritable gesture.

'What's the matter? Can I get you anything?' His hand sought hers anxiously across the table, but she slid hers away into her lap.

'It's nothing.' Oh what a lie — it was

everything. Her whole life was in a shambles all because of him.

Paul looked puzzled, anxious. 'But you said . . . '

'I know what I said, Paul,' she started deliberately. Stared at the table. Oh what was happening to her — to them?

'Look, I want to know, Sorelle.' There was an impatient irritation in his voice.

She glanced up at him. The frowning, commanding tanned face stared back into hers. His life was so calm, so ordered, everything running as he wanted. She wanted him to feel as she did, hopeless and in an emotional tangle. Wanted him to be hurt. Her words came quickly, low-voiced, her eyes flitting restlessly about the table. 'Things are easy for you, aren't they? Mutter a few dewy words and women fall at your feet. Do you ever think of them as people with feelings? I'm not something to be picked up whenever you want a change. You can't play about forever with . . . ' The word 'me' would not come from her tightened throat.

Looked up at him defiantly.

Paul sat straight in his chair, fingertips on the edge of the table. Anger had kindled in the now distant-looking eyes under the scowl, the brown warmth had gone from them. 'What d'you mean?' His voice was deep, slow with a hint of menace in it.

Sorelle had the strange feeling that the restaurant had emptied, they were there alone and the plushness and the magic of the place gone. Her jealousy was turning the man opposite her into a stranger. She knew it and yet could not stop herself. 'I — I saw you with Margot yesterday.'

He shrugged. 'I don't think that's anything I can be blamed for, after all she does work for me. If you must know we'd just been making final arrangements for her to take over the new Paris salon and shop — she is going to run it.'

'It was the way she was looking at you.'

Paul shrugged again. 'Naturally, she

was delighted with the opportunity to work full time in Paris. I was glad to be able to offer her the business. Not that she's short of money, but she likes the work — it's a challenge for her and she's a damned good model.'

It hadn't been that sort of look, Sorelle remembered, despising herself. Where was her pride, dignity?

'I've known her a long time, Sorelle,' Paul pointed out.

She twisted the knife already inside her, her tone accusatory. 'When you took me to Ormer Island you told me that I was the first woman you had taken to see it.'

'Yes,' he agreed, staring at her as if she were a stranger.

'You lied. There was lipstick on a cigarette in the house.' She watched him, sick at heart, saw the flicker of remembrance.

'All right, I made a mistake — I'd forgotten.' His jaw set. 'What does that make me? I'm damned if I'll be cross-examined.' A cruel and teasing smile touched his lips. 'I am a bachelor you know and what I do is my own affair.'

'That's a selfish attitude when it hurts others,' she riposted quickly. Hurried on, fighting to keep her voice steady. 'I'm not one of your worldly sophisticated people — I can't take your sort of game. Call me simple if you like.' He probably would, as she had been. 'As for this dress, I'll send it back to you. Perhaps it will do for your next conquest, or even for Mrs Melandes whoever she turns out to be,' she flung at him cuttingly.

He was as good as admitting it — he had not even bothered to deny that another woman had been there. Sorelle looked down at her hands twisted tightly together, cursing herself for venturing in to the no-man's land between them and getting hurt again. Would she never learn?

Paul pushed his chair back, the movement bringing the waiter hurrying to their table. He asked for the bill then stood up stern-faced. 'I'll take you home,' he said tersely.

'No thank you, I'll take a taxi,' she returned equally shortly.

'The car's outside.' He came round, held her chair away, his courteous action only serving to make her feel worse.

'I would prefer a taxi please if you don't mind, Paul.' He saw the flash of her eyes and shrugged. She wanted to be alone to bury her face and cry. Heard him tell the waiter to order one. Instead of making a scene she could have behaved in a more ladylike manner. He opened the door of the taxi for her and his polite and steady good night could quite easily have come from some hotel commissionaire.

She spent a wretched night, going over every detail of that disastrous evening time and time again. By the time morning came she had decided beyond doubt that she had been completely to blame for what had happened. She had been rude, insulting, and self-opinionated. Until her unfortunate and sudden change of attitude and manner, Paul had been charming and warm, seemingly delighting in her company. After being so generous and complimentary about her appearance he had not deserved such treatment. He had gone out of his way to make it a memorable evening for her. What had she done in return? Called him a liar. Shown a crude jealousy more fitting to a schoolgirl suffering from her first crush. A heavy dose of old-fashioned jealousy — that's what it had been. She recognised it now, but it was too late.

Her thoughts wandered on miserably. And as he had reminded her last night, he was a bachelor. There was no reason why he should not have met Margot even if it was nothing more than a business meeting. Also the identity of the woman who had left the cigarette had nothing to do with her. Sorelle realised that she had been far too possessive. She had behaved as if they were to be married. Humiliated herself.

She shuddered at the memory, remembered his look as he closed the taxi door after her. He would never contact her again. She had lost him, but one thing on which she was decided was that she must apologise. She recalled him saying that he was going away on the Monday — that was tomorrow.

Dressing quickly she found the *Privateer's* number — she had kept it from happier days, then went out to the phone booth. Perhaps he would refuse to speak with her and hang up on her. Nevertheless she must try. She gave the number to the operator, waited heavy-hearted, yet her pulse had quickened. Simply apologise, then ring off. It was ringing. She drew a tremulous breath as the receiver was picked up at the other end.

'The *Privateer* — Carlos speaking.' Carlos! She did not know whether to be glad or sorry. Had wanted to get it over with.

'Oh — oh Carlos, Sorelle Dalby here. Could I speak to Mr Melandes?' How formal she sounded — like a stranger.

'Ah, Miss Dalby.' He seemed pleased to hear from her. His delicious warm accents came again. 'Sorry, but Mr Melandes at island today.'

Well that was it then — she had tried. Wearily, sadly, she murmured dully, 'Thank you,' and was about to replace the receiver, when she caught his voice again.'

'The roses, Miss Dalby, I not able to get the roses for you.'

'Roses?' Roses? What was he talking about?

There was anxiety in Carlos' voice. 'Mr Melandes asked me to order roses — most important. I telephone shop — no answer. I think Mr Melandes forget it Sunday. Oh, Mr Melandes will be mad. I see you get them tomorrow eh?'

'For — for me,' she stammered.

'Yes. Mr Melandes say not to forget. I not forget but shop not open. You tell him Miss Dalby for me.'

'Don't you worry, Carlos. I'll back

you up — not your fault.'

Her feet were not touching the floor of the phone booth, she was floating in it. He had sent roses — had forgiven her. Oh, he was a big man inside as well as physically.

'Thank you, Miss Dalby.' Carlos sounded very relieved.

'The house is not connected yet with the phone?'

'No, but soon.'

'Never mind, it doesn't matter, Carlos.' An idea was forming in her mind. Carlos was going on again about the island, somebody visiting it and that was why Mr Melandes had gone over. But Sorelle wasn't listening. 'A million thanks, Carlos,' and jammed the receiver down. She felt like kissing the whole world.

It was just after ten o'clock. She had to be at work for three that day. If she got a move on she could just do it — hire a boat and go across to Ormer Island. Surprise Paul and make it up. After all he had told Carlos to send her some roses. She would meet his gesture half-way. In her new suddenly buoyant mood it seemed a marvellous idea. Gone was the dull miserable resignation of a few minutes before. Good old Carlos. If he hadn't said anything it might have been too late to see Paul who would be away for the next week.

Back in her flat she redressed quickly in the dress that she had worn the night before, it would please him to see her wearing it. She curled inside herself on remembering that she had said she would return it to him. Over it she threw her raincoat. The day was overcast and it would be cool on the water.

She drove faster into town than she had ever driven before. Then hurried along the esplanade looking for some-one to take her across to Ormer Island. The ferries were still running to Herm, Sark and Fermain Bay, but the season was nearing its end, the boats still moored and waiting to fill up with passengers. She enquired at the booking-office as to whether anyone was plying private hire.

The girl pointed down the slipway beyond the Herm boat to a white launch with a man busy in the stern. 'Bert down there — he will sometimes.'

Sorelle thanked her and made her way quickly down the slipway, praying that Bert would take her. He looked up as she reached the boat. A man of about sixty in a well-worn guernsey and faded blue peaked cap above a kindly large-nosed face from which blue eyes almost as blue as her own surveyed her. A cigarette dangled from the corner of his mouth. On her enquiry he looked critically with seaman's eyes at the sky then back at her anxiously-excited face. Guessed it must be very important and agreed.

The sea was calm and she was thankful for that, she didn't want to mark her surprise visit to Paul by being sick on her arrival. When they had gone about half-way Sorelle left the shelter of the cabin to sit in the stern. She was restless and becoming slightly nervous at the prospect of meeting Paul again unannounced as it were.

Occasionally she caught Bert's wondering glance at her. He was no doubt curious to know why she was going there. Perhaps he thought she was going to work at the house or that maybe she was a relation paying a visit, but the most likely, if he were aware of Paul's reputation, was that she was hurrying to his love nest — another hopeful in the Mrs Melandes contest.

As they drew near Sorelle saw a white yacht standing out from the southern part of the island. She was sure it was the *Privateer*, and a minute later she could make out the name on the stern. It was anchored just off the small beach — the one she recalled that he was going to name after her. There was no sign of anyone on the foreshore as the launch came to rest gently against the jetty. Sorelle clambered out and Bert retired into the cabin to wait for her. She had told him that she might be about half an hour.

9

She began to walk up the path towards the ridge of trees beyond which was the house. When she and Paul had visited the island those trees had been full-foliaged and green, their contours softer. She had, that clearly remembered day been locked in an embrace of desire with him on the hot sands, with little control left under his kisses and caresses. Now later in the year the baring branches were outlined darkly against the cloudy sky and she was alone. A momentary anxiety and uncertainty swept over her as to what kind of reception she would receive from him. It did not last long. He had instructed Carlos to send roses to her. That was not the action of a man who was unforgiving or who did not wish to see her again. Subconsciously her step quickened and she was unable to quell her mounting excitement. They could begin again as friends — take it from there. If that was the way he wanted it, so it would be. If she gave him time and did not rush him he may even get round to loving her some day.

Would he be in the house or maybe transferring some of his possessions to it from the yacht? What a surprise he would get when he saw her. In her imagination she saw his slow smile, expanding to one of delight. Perhaps they would not speak at once, just embrace. Then he would take her inside and they would talk about the future — a future without quarrels.

Reaching the line of trees she paused to look at the house and regain her breath. It appeared about the same except that the area in front of it had been cleared and tidied. Steps and terracing had been laid and the pool had been completely tiled. Sorelle started off down the slight incline to the house wondering whether she should stand and knock when she reached its door, or should she be bold and open it and announce herself? What a happy choice, contrasting sharply with the despair of the night before. Blessed Carlos for being instrumental in bringing she and Paul together again. If he had not mentioned the roses she would not have plucked up the courage to come.

A man and a woman appeared from behind the far end of the building and came slowly along the front of the house in her direction. The man with his arm around his companion's shoulders, she judging from her expression in contented and close conversation with him, he serious and concentrating on what she was saying.

Sorelle stopped dead, poised in mid-step unbelieving, her mind staggering at the sight. It was Paul and the dark-haired woman who had once accompanied him to the hotel restaurant! There was no mistaking her — it was the same woman. Rigid with shock she watched as they stopped and looked up at the house together. Then Paul hugged her and kissed her on the cheek before they walked up to the door, he in nodding agreement at something she said. She disappeared inside, and he followed, glancing behind casually. From twenty-five yards Sorelle and Paul regarded each other, he as if he had seen an apparition. She with bitter, bitter anguish numbing in its intensity, her world collapsing about her.

She turned, ran back up the path like a deer fleeing from the hunter over autumn leaves as brittle as her great love affair had now become.

'Sorelle. Wait — please wait,' he shouted and she heard him running after her.

She reached the trees. He caught up with her — grasped her arm. 'Wait. You don't understand.'

She turned on him in a fury, her eyes blazing the pain of mind engulfing her. 'Don't I?' she panted. 'God, I fell for it again. But I've finished waiting for you, I want no more.' Broke free from him, anger giving her strength. Raced down the path to the jetty sobbing brokenly. Almost fell into the boat, gasped at a surprised Bert to get her away as quickly as possible, then vanished into its cabin.

The engine note distorted the sound of Paul's voice as he reached the very end of the jetty. It didn't matter now, buried her face in her hands. How could he? Send her roses yet at the same time he was entertaining another woman on the island. He had thought he was safe. Making up to her with flowers and keeping her dangling, then looking for a new playmate. But was that all? Wasn't the truth even more hurtful? The intended roses, the presents, the clothes, the ill-fated dinner at the restaurant. Were they not all ways of saying goodbye? Letting her down lightly. And she in her naïvety had that afternoon brought extreme humiliation upon herself.

By the time she arrived back in her flat she had decided what she was going to do. Go to work as usual. She had an hour before she was due in at three o'clock. Give her notice of leaving — it was becoming a habit, and insist on finishing that night, even though she may lose money by not working a full notice. Then she would pay up to date for her flat and catch the first plane out of Guernsey on Monday for the mainland. There she would rejoin her mother and brother for the time being until she had sorted herself out.

One thing was certain, she could not stay in the island knowing that Paul Melandes was living close by. She had to get away — forget him. She rued the day that she had bumped into him. A kind of happiness and contentment had been hers up to then. Her life may not have been exciting but at least her heart was not constantly being wrenched apart, and her emotions dragged from peak to trough endlessly. She had been living on a knife edge. Now finally she had been cut — and severely.

At the hotel, from a strained and

agitated face, she told a concerned manager her decision was for personal reasons. A touch of wry and dismal humour bubbled through — it was the second time she had given in her notice in a few weeks. He was kind and thoughtful, paid her what she was owed and promised a reference any time she required one.

It was done, she had made the break, and spent the rest of the time at reception in a kind of stupor, performing her duties automatically. Once a call came from the *Privateer*. She recognised the American voice, slammed the phone down immediately. Glad and relieved when it was time to finish. She hadn't wanted to say goodbye to others of the staff and had kept quiet about her leaving. What a way to go. But better to cut herself off from the island life — make it final.

A sad and miserable night became an equally sad and miserable morning. She rang the airport early to find that the only seat she could get was on the plane leaving that evening at six o'clock. The next thing she did was to take her car to the garage she had bought it from. It wasn't a princely sum they gave her for it, but it would help with her finances until she got a job on the mainland. It was one more link with her birthplace severed.

Then later that morning she went to Le Gouffre with its high cliffs and lonely paths. She felt she would have gone mad if she had stayed in the flat until it was time to go to the airport. Le Gouffre was the one place she and Paul had never visited together, the others held so many memories. She sat alone on a seat overlooking the sea. Later the sun broke through, sparkling the water, and the gulls with their haunting cries skimmed the waves and played round the headland. Afterwards, lost in her troubles and spirits at a low ebb, she had a bean-jar — broad beans in hot soup with crusty bread at a little café situated in a hollow at the rear of the cliffs, then caught the bus back to her flat to pick up her bags.

Her neighbour, a woman from the next flat, intercepted her. A man — an American in a big silver car had been enquiring after Sorelle. She pointed to the roses placed by the door. He had left those. Sorelle thanked her and took the flowers inside. A note was attached. Savagely she tore it up without reading it, then threw the cellophane wrapped bouquet into the rubbish bin. Sick at heart with herself and everything, she was determined that she was not going to fall for that trick again. But how it all could have been so different.

She checked her bags into the airport just before five o'clock. An hour to kill before take off. Decided to freshen herself up. Looked into the mirror in the ladies' room, saw her unhappy face and returned to the airport lounge. There through the large window she watched the occasional plane come and go. She became restless, wanting to be away. Her watch said five-twenty. Only that? Made her way towards the book stall. Anything to pass the time. Two people were in front of her as she approached it. Pausing before her turn, she glanced round. Stared in disbelief. Paul Melandes was bearing down on her, stern and determined-faced! Shocked, she turned and hurried away in the direction of the lounge again. Why had he come? Did he have to be so cruel? Couldn't he leave her in her misery — he had caused her enough already.

'Sorelle.' The voice was commanding yet held a plea. She rounded on him, uncaring of the people about. 'Leave me alone. Get away from me. You've ruined my life. I hate you. I never want to see you again as long as I live. You had your chance long ago. Nothing you say now will alter things. Goodbye.' Glad to see the hurt in his eyes before she half ran from him. He had received some of his own medicine. She stumbled into the bar area — anywhere to hide herself. The sight of him had opened the wound in her heart again before it had had the ghost of a chance to heal. Bowed her head over her hands at an empty table unmindful of the curious looks thrown her way.

Dully she heard the announcement that passengers for the mainland must now go through the departure gate. Sorelle lifted her head. Soon it would be all over and the sickness called love would fade and die. It seemed impossible but others had said it would. In time she would forget.

Somebody had left a newspaper on the table. It lay front page up — unrolled and new — that evening's *Guernsey Press*. The large black print caught her eye. 'Millionaire to quit island. Mr Melandes, millionaire buyer of Ormer Island only a few weeks ago, is leaving. Finds it impossible to carry out his original plans. Pictured below with Mr Melandes is Mrs Rose Hessler, his sister, who had been staying with him recently.' Sorelle's hands screwed the page sides. The face of the woman staring at her was the same woman who had been with Paul on the island yesterday.

His sister! The same person who had accompanied him that night at the hotel restaurant! Emotions that could not be counted ravaged Sorelle's brain. Oh God! What had she done? Sent the man she loved away — forever. It was all a ghastly mistake.

No dignity left she knocked the table aside in her eagerness to catch Paul before it was too late. Perhaps it was already. Would he ever forgive her? The terrible things she had said. Oh where was he? Her eyes scanned the interior of the building feverishly. She saw him making for the airport doors. Prayed — 'please let me catch him. Don't let him go. Tell him I'm sorry. I love him.'

He turned at the dashing feet behind him. She waved the paper clutched in her hand at him like a mad thing. The last few yards. 'Your sister,' she cried, 'I didn't know. I thought — oh . . . ' She shuddered in his suddenly wide open welcoming arms. 'My bloody mistake,' she sobbed against him. 'Oh, how can you forgive me?' They stood enfolded together, oblivious of everyone else.

'Forgive you, Sorelle my dearest. No — no — not forgive — love, Sorelle, that's what I'm trying to tell you, you little idiot, you brave, independent, wonderful thing. I love you — I love you — I love you.' Her ears were cradled in the glorious sound of the words she thought would never come from the man who now crushed her to him.

In a haze she knew she was being taken back to the *Privateer*. Found herself sitting with Paul to a meal prepared by Carlos looking on beamingly and happily. Then somehow without them being aware he disappeared, leaving them alone.

She and Paul talked and held on to each other. 'My sister,' he explained, 'had come to give me encouragement and hope — hope that you would see me again. I was showing her over the house I was preparing for you.' He sighed in anger at himself. 'I was so stubborn in the restaurant I could have

\t\old you there and then that she had been to the island.' He looked down tenderly at her. 'Will you ever forgive me?'

'Forgive you?' She half shook her head that he could doubt it. Her eyes told him all. She snuggled up to him still in a dream from which she hoped she would never awake. Felt his heart beating against her cheek and also the shiver that ran through him as he spoke against her hair.

'I don't wonder you doubted me. I had lost the ability to feel love. I was an outcast of my own making, thinking that I should never really love someone again unselfishly. When love in the shape of you confronted me I failed to recognise it. What a fool I was — a blind pleasure-seeking fool.' His words flowed over her, enfolding her in a cocoon of contentment. 'Do you remember,' he continued, 'that day on the island — that wonderful day when we picnicked by the water?'

'How could I forget it?'

'Well I meant to ask you to marry me then, but I lost my nerve thinking that you might not take me seriously, knowing I was sure, of my reputation.'

Sorelle turned her head up to him. 'I would have married you that very day I first bumped into you. I loved you even from then.'

She was surprised when he gently disengaged himself and stood up holding his hands out to her. 'In that case, come with me.'

Puzzled but happy she allowed him to lead her out on to the after deck. It had been raining and a rainbow joined the sea and town. He pointed at the town church then towards Ormer Island. 'Will you marry me there my darling Sorelle, and let me take you to live on Ormer Island?' He drew her tenderly and protectively in his arms, held her face up to his with his fingertips. 'There would be no life for me now if you refused.' His eyes searched hers with a glowing expectancy and desire. Her legs were almost incapable of supporting her as she sighed her very willing answer.

He bent and picked her up easily into his arms and carried her inside, their lips joined together in a long burning kiss. Just momentarily her eyes flickered open, seeing the rainbow again — a bridge over her former doubts and fears. A rainbow of love.

THE END

VISIONS OF THE HEART

Christine Briscomb

When property developer Connor Grant contracted Natalie Jensen to landscape the grounds of his large country house near Ashley in South Australia, she was ecstatic. But then she discovered he was acquiring — and ripping apart — great swathes of the town. Her own mother's house and the hall where the drama group met were two of his targets. Natalie was desperate to stop Connor's plans — but she also had to fight the powerful attraction flowing between them.

THE GYPSY'S RETURN

Sara Judge

After the death of her cruel father, Amy Keene's stepbrother and stepsister treated her just as badly. Amy had two friends, old Dr. Hilland and the washerwoman, Rosalind, with her fatherless child Becky. When Rosalind falls ill, Amy is entrusted with a letter to be given to Becky on her marriage. When the letter's contents are discovered, it causes Amy both mental and physical suffering and sets the seal of fate upon Rosalind's gypsy friend, Elias Jones.

WEB OF DECEIT

Margaret McDonagh

A good-looking man turned up on Louise's doorstep one day, introducing himself as Daniel Kinsella, an Australian friend of her brother-in-law, Greg. He said he had come to stay whilst he did some research — apparently Greg had written to her about it. Louise's initial reaction was to turn him away, but he was very persuasive. However, she was to discover that Daniel had bluffed his way into her life, and soon she found herself caught up in his dangerous mission.